W0246751

PENGUIN BOOKS
CURFEW IN THE CITY

Vibhuti Narain Rai, a social activist and educationist, completed his master's in English literature from Allahabad University in 1971 and joined the Indian Police Service in 1975. In his thirty-six years' eventful career, he was awarded the Police Medal for Meritorious Service and the President's Police Medal for Distinguished Service, and was posted as senior sub-inspector and inspector general of police in several communally sensitive areas of Uttar Pradesh. An accomplished novelist, Rai's *Ghar*, *Kissa Loktantra*, *Tabadala* and *Prem Ki Bhootkatha* received critical acclaim. *Curfew in the City*, originally published in Hindi as *Shahar Mein Curfew*, invited the wrath of Hindutva forces that even demanded a ban on it. Rai retired as the vice chancellor of Mahatma Gandhi Antarrashtriya Hindi Vishwavidyalaya, Wardha.

C.M. Naim is professor emeritus of Urdu studies at the University of Chicago. He has also published translations of novellas by Qurratulain Hyder and satires by Harishankar Parsai.

Vibhuti Narain Rai

CURFEW IN THE CITY

A Novella

PENGUIN BOOKS

An imprint of Penguin Random House

PENGUIN BOOKS

USA | Canada | UK | Ireland | Australia
New Zealand | India | South Africa | China | Singapore

Penguin Books is part of the Penguin Random House group of companies
whose addresses can be found at global.penguinrandomhouse.com

Published by Penguin Random House India Pvt. Ltd
4th Floor, Capital Tower 1, MG Road,
Gurugram 122 002, Haryana, India

First published in Hindi as *Shahar Mein Curfew* by Sahitya Upkram 1998
Published by Penguin Books India 2016

ISBN 9780143065586

Typeset in Dante MT Std by by Maniworks.com, New Delhi

Printed at Repro India Limited

www.penguin.co.in

CONTENTS

FOREWORD

During 1947, as the independent nations of Pakistan and India appeared on the political map of the world, violence in the name of religion reached unprecedented magnitude in South Asia. It abated considerably in the 1950s but since then has steadily grown worse. In Pakistan, where non-Muslims were too few to matter much, Muslim communal passion was first directed against the Ahmadi Muslims, but gradually took on more varied ethnic and sectarian dimensions, pitting the Deobandis against the Barelavis, the Sunnis against the Shiahs, the Sindhis against the Muhajirs and so on. More recently, however, even the miniscule Christian and Hindu populations in Punjab and Sindh have become its victims. In Bangladesh, with its still substantial non-Muslim population, anti-Hindu and anti-Chakma actions by the Muslim majority and by the state itself, have continued without much relief. And in India, where the Muslim minority is large enough to account for almost 12 per cent of the population, the phrase 'communal riots' has come to be a euphemism for anti-Muslim pogroms directed by certain elements in the majority Hindu community—with the encouragement, even active participation, of those very agencies of the state that are expected to protect the victims. Jabalpur, Jamshedpur, Muradabad, Bhiwandi, Hashimpura and Maliana, Bhagalpur, Baroda and Ahmedabad, and most recently Surat and Bombay of 1993—these are only the most haunting signposts on India's path of steady decline as a civil polity. To which list we should also add Delhi and Kanpur in the dark days of 1984, when similar pogroms were directed against the Sikhs.

In response to the communal violence at the time of the Partition, a massive body of literature was produced in Bengali, Hindi, Punjabi and—what I directly know—Urdu. Urdu writers on both sides of the new international border produced countless short stories and several novels about those times. One critical issue they faced was: how does one create a piece of fiction about a reality so horrible? Some responded by doing a 'balancing act'—if five victims of one religious persuasion were mentioned in the beginning, they were matched by five victims belonging to the other religion at the end. Some also felt that to bring the warring communities together they must put the final blame on a common enemy: the erstwhile colonial rulers. Other writers wrote as partisans; they saw their own community as being only a victim, and blamed the other community for being the exclusive perpetrator of violence. Most of these writings emphasized the 'magnitude' of the violence—the killings, the rapes, the destruction of property, the uprooting of populations. Only a small corpus explored the truly horrific—the casual betrayals, the meanness and cruelty in seemingly ordinary acts, the human capacity to routinize inhumanity—the evil in the 'banal'. Saadat Hasan Manto in his stories of the Partition riots neither blamed any single group nor tried to distribute the blame equally. His significance and the lasting power of his stories lie in his focusing on those moments when a man, despite having done horrible things, could be shown as still being capable of doing ordinary little things. This strategy did not lessen the horror of the man's actions; in fact, it enhanced it by making them the acts of someone not unlike us. At the same time, it made it possible to envision some hope, some capacity in mankind that could be harnessed to fight against such horrors.

The hatred and violence of 1947 was blamed by most writers at the time on the machinations of our erstwhile colonial rulers. Almost all of them felt that to bring the Hindus and Muslims together they had to find a common enemy in the English. But the events of the 1970s and the 1980s are different. We must face the fact that 'the enemy is us'. To my knowledge, literary responses to contemporary communal violence in the sub-continent have not been extensive in any of the three countries and their many languages. For example, in Urdu in India, there are any number of short stories and poems about the present plight of the Muslims, but there are no major novels, anthologies or special issues of magazines. Likewise, I know of no work of imagination in Urdu from Pakistan that tries to explore the trajectory that communal violence has taken there.

In fact, in the sub-continental perspective, one can cite only two books that have made a significant impact in this area: *Lajja (Shame)* in Bengali, by the Bangladeshi writer Taslima Nasrin, and *Shahar Mein Curfew (Curfew in the City)* in Hindi, by Vibhuti Narain Rai. Nasrin's book gained immediate notice in South Asia and abroad due to the fatwa issued against the author. Rai's book has remained much less known even in India, though it did generate the wrath of some votaries of Hindutva, who successfully prevented it from being made into a film. Both Nasrin and Rai have written about the persecution of minority communities by the majority communities to which they themselves belong in their respective countries. Otherwise, the two books are very different.

Nasrin's linear narrative covers thirteen days in the life of a Hindu family in Dhaka in 1992 with considerable speed and passion; it also contains lengthy segments of a purely documentary nature. The latter generally dismayed reviewers in Bangladesh and India. But the novelist Amitav Ghosh more accurately understood the aims of Nasrin's narrative when he wrote in the *Telegraph* of 24 June 1994: '. . . taken on its own terms, the book's strength can be seen to lie precisely in what appear to be its formal weakness. In its breakneck urgency, its direct and unembellished Bengali prose, in the narrative inseparability of its fictional and documentary material, in its polemical repetitiveness and its undisguised emotional immediacy.' He then went on to compare Nasrin with the Egyptian feminist Nawal El Saadawi, and argued that the two 'have pioneered one of the most powerful forms of our times. The polemiction—polemical fictions that are perhaps the most appropriate possible literary response to the oppressive banality of contemporary religious extremism.' In another way too, these documentary sections are exactly what makes *Lajja* so significant. They give names and professions and homes to those who otherwise get mentioned only as anonymous statistics. Nasrin wishes us not to forget those ordinary details that make these victims of communal fanaticism not unlike their enemies—in the end, so like us.

Rai's novella is not 'polemiction'. It is, in fact, quite modest in ambition and execution. Though begun in 1980, in response to a riot in Allahabad that he personally observed as the senior superintendent of police there, the book came out only in 1988. Its episodic narrative covers three days in the life of a small neighbourhood in Allahabad in the grip of a curfew during the riot. Divided into nine short chapters, it alternates between the story of Sayeeda, the wife of a bidi-maker, and her family, claustrophobic in effect in being confined to their one-room house, and other simultaneous events that take place elsewhere. That 'elsewhere' is spatially more open and varied, but—affected by the curfew—equally distorted and horrifying. The two progressions meet in the penultimate chapter, where a police party conducts 'searches' in Muslim homes—the home of a nationalist lawyer, Sayeeda's home and the palatial compound of the Haji. At the end of the book, the curfew continues.

Despite a few instances of authorial interventions, Rai seems to strive for a cool, sometimes ironic and detached voice. Nevertheless, he too wants us to come close to the victims of violence and persecution through our knowledge of their ordinariness. Thus Sayeeda, perhaps the central character in his novella, is not just a grief-stricken mother whose baby daughter dies during the curfew but also a rural person who hates using the latrine in her new home in the city.

Rai's narrative is not about the 'riot' itself, or rather, it is not about the killing and pillaging and raping, the events that were very much the focus of the narratives of the stories that were written about the riots of 1946 and 1947. It is not a story of people gone barbaric in the heat of a moment of passion or revenge. It is about cold, calculated greed and blind, senseless hatred.

Consider the chapter on 'rape'. One may say that Rai is being too artful. The girl remains without a name, so do her assailants. But consider what has been told implicitly. Her family has the values that encourage education for girls, but not the resources to maintain those values safely. Her mother sews clothes for a dealer; she has to look after her younger siblings and do all the housework. She has an 'affair' with a young man from her neighbourhood, but we are told what inevitably happened in such 'affairs'. She is knitting a sweater for the boy from some worn and discarded wool. He hopes to buy her a shawl by taking out some money from the little he earns and—according to his values—must put in his mother's hands. Theirs is not a romance that would shake the world, not something that bards would sing about. The girl goes to school on the fateful day, against the wishes of her mother; the boy does not stir out, obedient to his mother's command. The girl is also abandoned by the school authorities who make no effort to send the girls home safely. (But did they have the needed resources?) Running in panic, the girl finds herself in a lane that—in her panic—looks strange to her but is in fact not far from her own alley. There, three men, hiding for safety in their milling shop, drag her inside and rape her. She calls them *bhaiya* ('brothers'), they call themselves 'sister-fuckers'. The incident is seen by others, but no one comes to help the girl. Fearful, they are themselves cowering in their meagre homes. In a milieu where a name indicates the person's religion and much more, Rai has a clear purpose in keeping the victim and the assailants nameless.

More complex but similar in intentions is the chapter with Devi Lala, the neighbourhood drunk. Here we are told that the lane is 'Hindu'. Of course, its physical condition turns out to be not too different from the neighbouring 'Muslim' lane—they perhaps share the same filthy, open sewer. But in the 'Hindu' lane, the residents are free to move. Stragglers come home, bringing incredible tales of Muslim atrocities. Gossip flows. The local drunk gains a respectability that he had not known before. Then a police party arrives; it demands and receives hospitality from the residents. The children who had earlier shouted out doggerel about Devi Lala, now run around shouting a slogan declaring solidarity between the police and the Hindus, making the Muslims their common enemy. Meanwhile, a different, more ordinary drama has been going on at one end of the lane, where some of the local lotharios are waiting to flirt with the daughters of the only local Muslim resident, a tailor. Their impatience makes them throw a rock at the tailor's door. The noise causes a general panic. When the truth dawns on the elders of the lane they suddenly become aware of the tailor's presence in their midst. They want to reassure him but he never opens his door. Then they recall that he had done that in every previous riot. Now the children take up another slogan, left over from the elections held not too long ago, and turn it into a declaration of solidarity with the tailor, Yusuf.

Most of the narrative is about the death and burial of Sayeeda's daughter. The little girl dies of cholera, but she also dies because she couldn't get proper medicine, because she lived in terrible conditions where survival was almost impossible. She died, as had so many other children in that family and in that neighbourhood. But the curfew that deprived her of better medical treatment, now almost deprives her of a proper burial. Her grandfather has to risk his body, even life, to go and get curfew passes to take the dead body to the graveyard in the morning. Her grandmother has to take similar risks to fetch water from the public tap in order to wash the corpse. In fact, the tiny corpse barely escapes being crushed under the boots of the police party that is going around 'doing searches' for weapons.

The riot itself is not mentioned at all. There is only the briefest mention of some small explosive device being thrown against a temple wall that causes no damage. But immediately the existing fears and suspicions take over, a curfew is imposed by the authorities, and the city becomes divided into 'Muslim' and 'Hindu' neighbourhoods.

The narrative focuses on how the curfew affects the simple, mundane matters in the lives of ordinary people: a sick child cannot get medicine; a family cannot get drinking water; a girl cannot walk down the street in safety; people cannot even stay indoors in security; a dead child cannot easily be given a decent burial. But political and civic leaders and journalists and authorities go on living their lives of privilege. They do not lose their privileges. The underprivileged are denied even the little they had. There is a nexus of interests among the leaders, the journalists, and the authorities.

The role of the police and the PAC is separated from that of the BSF and the army, as has often been mentioned in the narratives of the victims of riots in the past. The police force is shown to contain blatantly communal personnel, both in high and low positions. There do not seem to be any Muslims in the bureaucracy, civil or police. Also missing are ideologues and rabble rousers of the type often mentioned with reference to communalistic political parties. But their presence is felt in the background. We see the authorities in action as they conduct searches and hold a peace committee meeting. The flagrant criminality of the searches is in marked contrast to the utter hypocrisy and self-serving nature of the peace committee proceedings. We know that both activities will be reported in the official record as well as in the journalists' accounts, but not the way the author has shown them.

It is not an ambitious book. One may even call it slight. Hindi literary critics pointed out its journalistic quality. The author himself was not unaware of it. In an interview in 1991, he remarked, 'I concede that it appears to be more a piece of reportage than fiction proper—reflective and contemplative. In part this is a consequence of haste, but it was also deliberate. I wanted it to assume a certain form. I should like to think, however, that given more time and effort [it] would have become a better work of art.'

What, nevertheless, makes it deserving of our fullest attention is one simple fact: in this novel, the author and the citizen have become one. Also, it is, after all, an insider's narrative. This is not a left-handed compliment. In a society where literacy is not so common, where citizens of India have fought in two world wars and at least three other wars but have yet to produce one novel, one poem written by someone who actually went through those wars, where hardly any bureaucrat or academician or doctor has produced a book of imaginative literature dealing with his particular profession or milieu, we should be grateful that now a police officer has written a novel about something which involved him professionally. He remembered what he saw. That is the main thing. Forgetfulness is the worst crime in these times when history and memory are both being suppressed or distorted for instant gratification of the worst kind—and at a cost to those who have remained unmentioned in conventional chronicles, or mentioned only as statistics, nameless, even bodiless.

The book went through two editions in three years, and in March 1991 a journalist in Allahabad announced his plans to make a feature film based on it. It was this announcement that brought forth a 'fatwa' from Shri Ashok Singhal, the secretary-general of the Vishwa Hindu Parishad. Not surprisingly, he had not even bothered to read the book, for he advised Mr Rai to resign from the government service *before* publishing his book. More effectively, he threatened to burn down any cinema house that would dare to show the proposed film. Though Hindi literati came out in full force to denounce the threat, the film was never made.

In conclusion, it is worth noting that Rai, after finishing the novel, did not complacently sit back. Instead, he took time out from his professional work to do research on the violent behaviour of the police in Indian civil life as a whole. It should also be noted with some satisfaction that his research was supported by the National Police Academy. Some of his findings and reflections are included in the afterword he specially wrote for this book.

May 1996

PREFACE TO THIS EDITION

Having co-existed in India for more than a thousand years, Hindus and Muslims have forged an amazing saga of human relationship. On the one hand, it has resulted in great creativity in the fields of art, music, architecture and sculpture but on the other, it has produced a sad narrative of conflicts and tribulations.

Both communities have lived together all these years and contributed to making life beautiful but they have also fought bitterly. Two hundred years of British hegemony drove the wedge between the two communities deeper. In fact, it is largely owing to the intervention of the British that the cooperation between Hindus and Muslims took a beating and areas of conflict widened. The result was the Partition, planned and executed on the premise that Hindus and Muslims should comprise two different nations, thus validating religion as the basis of nationhood. Fortunately, the leadership of newly independent India, which was struggling to develop the country into a nation state, could sense the hollowness of this doctrine and rejected it outright.

The Constitution of India declares it a secular state. No particular religion, not even that of the overwhelming majority, enjoys the status of state religion. The Constitution guarantees freedom of religion to every individual and ensures that religious minorities have the unhindered right not only to follow their own religion but also to propagate it.

On the ground, however, reality often appears to be different. Time and again the state and society fail to negotiate on the issue of pluralities: religious, sociocultural, linguistic, regional and so on. The apparent contradiction between centralized polity and politicized diversities further complicates and compounds the problem. One of the saddest realities of the sexagenarian Indian secular democracy is frequent communal fights between Hindus and Muslims. Every few years we witness incidents of sheer barbarism coupled with callous state empathy. Is this because we could not integrate secularism as part of our culture despite such a long association with the West? Secularism in India was for a long time regarded as a western import incompatible with our way of life. Nehru articulated the idea of secularism as equal respect to all religions. To him, religion was a matter of personal belief which had absolutely no role in the functioning of the state. Unfortunately the Indian state has faltered on this count more frequently than not. The minorities harbour a general impression that during the communal riots of the recent past the state did not do enough to protect the people affected by it. Commissions of inquiry to probe into the causes and assign responsibility were set up mechanically but the guilty seldom got punished. It sends out a dangerous message to society as it seems to signal the presence of a bipolar law.

This novella narrates the story of a curfew-bound town in northern India but it could just as well be the experience of any Indian settlement. The relationship or rather the strain in the relationship between the state and minorities is conspicuous during any incident of communal violence. The pain, suffering and sense of alienation that such violence brings with it can be perceived on human faces like the proverbial writing on the wall. It has been almost three decades since the publication of the first edition but it seems that the situation is more or less the same today. After the multiple editions and translation into more than a dozen languages that this book has seen, I feel that if I write again to recount the suffering of people locked and suffocated in their squalid households in townships during rigidly enforced curfews, it might be a repetition.

Noida
October 2015

ACKNOWLEDGEMENTS

The translator would like to thank the friend who first brought the book to his attention in its Urdu translation. Next he would like to express his gratitude to the author, who provided the Hindi text, read the translation with care, answered all queries, and willingly agreed to provide a valuable Afterword. Lastly, he must thank an old and dear friend, Carlo Coppola, for improving his English.

This translation is gratefully dedicated to Vibhuti Narain Rai and Taslima Nasrin.

1

The curfew came as no surprise. At least that part of the city where a curfew was declared every other year or so had been readying itself—mentally and physically—the entire preceding week. The air almost crackled, and experienced people who could recognize tension in just one deep breath knew a curfew would soon be declared. In fact, they couldn't understand why it had been postponed for so long.

The rioting started around 1.30 p.m. By 1.45 p.m., police vehicles equipped with loudspeakers were rushing around the city announcing the curfew. Of course, by then, that was merely a formality. Already in barely fifteen minutes, G.T. Road, from the vegetable market of Khuldabad to the Bahdurganj neighbourhood, had become almost empty. Only a few shopkeepers and some women who had been separated from their menfolk in the panic of the moment could still be seen fleeing in terror down the road.

This riot, which occurred in the last week of August, had already been rehearsed in June; consequently people didn't need to be told what to do. Their first task was to quickly pull the store shutters down; then dropping all else, they were to flee their homes through alleys and by-lanes. And they did exactly that, leaving behind abandoned bicycles, slippers, shoes, bags, what have you. In just the shortest while, busy streets like G.T. Road, Katju Road, Mirza Ghalib Road and Nurullah Road were totally deserted. Only at the mouths of some of the lanes could one still see small clusters of people; at the sight of the police they would run back into the lanes, then gather again after the police moved on.

Sounds of gunshots were still coming from Minhajpur, behind the Shahganj police outpost, and from Gulab Bari, beyond Mansur Park. In addition, occasional shots could be heard from inside lanes and from Akbarpur, Nihalpur and Mirza Ghalib Road. By 2 p.m., the army had moved in and taken positions along the Shahganj–Nurullah road and Maulana Shaukat Ali Marg. Then, around 2.30 p.m., raindrops began to fall, and soon became a steady downpour. That calmed everything down. By 3 p.m. the 'game' was over, and people had resigned themselves to huddling inside their homes.

Outside, in the streets, there was only fear—and the police—and torrents of rain bringing relief from August's wretched heat.

In the space of ninety minutes, six persons had been killed, thirty to forty wounded, and close to 300 taken into custody. It was as if some monstrous bird of prey, whirling above the city, had suddenly pounced upon it and ripped it apart, then, grasping the pieces in its claws, had flown up high only to fling them back to the ground. Now the city lay horribly torn and bloodied. What that hour and a half had done was going to take much, much longer to be undone.

This seems to be what had happened. Around 1.30 p.m. that afternoon, a handful of boys came out of a lane near the Bank of Baroda's branch office at the intersection of Mirza Ghalib Road and G.T. Road. They threw a hand bomb at the wall of a temple near the Gariwan Tola, then ran back into the lane. In fact, what exploded on the temple wall was more like a firecracker than a bomb. It only made a very loud noise, and caused no damage or injury. But, because it had been thrown at a temple wall, Hindu bystanders concluded that the perpetrators could only have been Muslims. They immediately started attacking every Muslim who came that way. The first target was three people on a motorcycle. When the motorcycle was blocked and brought crashing down, one of the three jumped up and ran away. The other two remained kneeling on the road, covering their heads with their hands; they were kicked and stoned until a police party from nearby Ahmadganj rescued them. Other passers-by were also similarly attacked.

Meanwhile, on the nearby Mirza Ghalib Road, scattered groups of excited young men began throwing stones at the various security men posted along the street. Soon, one could see those Home Guards and policemen fleeing towards the Gariwan Tola. As they ran towards the Bank of Baroda office—where some PAC and police had already arrived—they had to protect their heads from the stones thrown by the boys and men milling at every corner where a lane branched off from the road. One of the fleeing men fell down about a hundred yards from the bank, his face cut up by shards of glass. He got up again and, covering his face with both hands, kept running. Suddenly, in his desperate blind rush, he crashed into a cluster of boys gathered at one of the lanes. He had barely staggered away from them when a dagger hit his left side and pierced through his ribs. He struggled a few more steps, then collapsed in the middle of the road.

At various places in the city, there were explosions and gunshots—almost simultaneously. It seemed as if it had all been planned, that some invisible hand was behind the incidents. Everywhere, hand bombs were exploded, but no one was injured. Their purpose, it seemed, was to create a special aura of terror, and in that they succeeded immensely.

For some time now there had been a rumour that Muslims were making preparations to attack the police. The dread of such an attack had grasped the heart of the average policeman. There had been other riots in the western part of the state in which several Muslims had died from police bullets. That, the rumour claimed, was why the Muslims were angry. It was said that if Muslims found any policeman alone in their neighbourhood, they wouldn't leave him alive. Consequently, in the past couple of days, no policeman had gone into the Muslim areas alone or even with just one more man. Whenever a need arose, the police had always gone fully armed and in groups of four or five, including a sub-inspector.

No one had been injured in most of these explosions and gunfire incidents. In several places, the police had been in the open, but the bomb had exploded ten or fifteen yards away from them, to their right or left, against some wall. In each instance, however, it was immediately assumed that the bomb had been thrown by a Muslim. There promptly followed a search of all the Muslim households in the area. At most places nothing was found. But at some, the police came across knives used for dressing meat or licensed arms that had not been turned in to the authorities despite previous orders. The men of such households were instantly taken into custody under either

Section 25 of the Arms Act or Section 188 of the Indian Penal Code.

By the time the rain ceased around 3.30 p.m. it had brought some relief from the heat—and from the equally oppressive tension. The journalists who set out in police jeeps expecting to have a 'picnic' were disappointed to find the streets totally empty. Only police vehicles were around, dashing this way or that. If there was any 'tension' in the city it was not visible on its streets.

But earlier, before the rain had entirely stopped, a number of police vans came speeding from different directions and stopped near the Shahganj police outpost. There were a few uniformed men inside the police outpost, anxiously peering out of the windows; otherwise, all the way to the Eye Hospital and the nurses' hostel, it was utter desolation. The rain had slowed but kept coming back in sudden bursts, which made the scene look more desolate and terrifying. A little earlier, the police had fired several rounds in that area; now the tense silence of their effect lay heavy over everything.

The vans disgorged two superintendents of police, one deputy superintendent, and a handful of inspectors and sub-inspectors. Some of them sought shelter from the drizzle in a nearby veranda; the rest simply stood in a circle on the road in front of the police outpost and talked about what their next step should be. The control room had informed them of the firing. On seeing the new arrivals, the policemen inside the outpost also drifted out and joined them.

Constantly interrupting each other, and in highly agitated voices, what they told the officers was simply this: twenty minutes earlier, there had been an incident of police firing—a mob had showered stones on the police, with the result that the

5

latter had had to climb on to the roof of a building to open fire on the attackers. The neighbourhood behind the police outpost was communally mixed. It was utterly quiet now, but only a little bit earlier, frightening cries and other noises could be heard from that direction. The policemen were certain that some houses there had been attacked.

The new arrivals finally decided to go into the lanes and see for themselves. Nothing was to be gained from standing there on the road. If even one man had been killed or one house set on fire, the consequences could be very serious. So far no incident had been of the kind that could set off a major communal outburst, but once incidents of arson and stabbing started in the lanes, nothing could stop them.

The two SPs conferred amongst themselves for several minutes, then, with a shrug, they set off down the side street. They were followed by a group of men from the PAC and the regular police. Minhajpur was a neighbourhood built around a small park and had mainly two- or three-storeyed homes of well-to-do Muslims. It did not have the filth and poverty of the other chiefly Muslim areas.

Persistent rain and the all-encompassing desolation had created an atmosphere that made even the jawans startle every so often at the sound of their own boots against the pavement. The junior officers had their handguns out; the jawans had their rifles ready. All the guns were aimed high, for on every roof or balcony they feared an enemy. Their tense fingers curled around the triggers. Any nervous finger could have created another incident of police firing. Every few moments, the officers loudly whispered to their men to keep their rifles pointing upwards. As they proceeded onwards, they took shelter behind the pillars and porches of the houses. They were deeply frightened people; each one of them carried in his mind an enemy whom he kept glimpsing on various balconies or at the next intersection. But before his gun could respond, the enemy would vanish again.

They came upon their first sign of success when they arrived close to where the park came to an end. At the very tip of the park, a dark splash of blood lay on the road; someone had tried to preserve it by encircling it with pieces of bricks. Persistent rain, however, had made the blood run beyond the circle. It was still possible to see where someone must have collapsed after being hit by a bullet, for in the centre there remained a big clot of blood, which the drizzle even now was eating into, causing thin, red lines to run in many directions.

The senior officers gathered around to examine the present state of the blood. The rest, firmly gripping their guns, kept their eyes fixed on the porches and balconies around them. The rain was pounding down, and a veil seemed to have fallen over everything, making it difficult to discern what any odd shape on a balcony might be. And yet, if one tried very hard, one could see that on every balcony or porch there was someone, hiding behind a pillar or peeping through a window. Fingers twisted around the triggers would harden. Eyes would fix on that menacing figure. And then they would discover that they were mistaken—like every other time—and their fingers would slowly relax again.

After noting the direction in which the blood had spread, the officers set off down a lane that began near the edge of the park. A muddied red line clearly indicated that someone had been dragged away down that lane. But every door they passed was bolted, and the rain and the total lack of any other sound made it impossible to decide which house the wounded person might

7

have been taken to. Their only hope lay in that thin, almost washed out, red line on the paving stones.

The lanes spread out like a forbidding labyrinth. Before any lane ended it split off into at least three more lanes. The clouded sky and the rain falling in sheets had turned midday brightness into early dusk. In the dark and stuffy lanes, the searchers found it difficult to perform their two tasks: follow the thin line of blood, while protecting themselves from an imagined enemy. The senior officers in front were looking for traces of blood; the men following them had their rifles and handguns aimed at the roofs and balconies. The surrounding walls protected them from being hit directly in the face by bursts of rain; nevertheless, they were all drenched from cap to boot.

One officer suddenly stopped. A second pricked his ears and stood still, listening. Some of the other men noticed the two taut faces and looked around, then, huddling against the walls, tried to figure out what was happening.

Disturbing the rain-drenched stillness came soft wafts of someone wailing. Everyone became alert. Silently but deliberately, they began to move in the direction of the sound. After just a few steps, the sound became more distinct.

It was a most curious kind of wailing, as if several women were trying to cry out their grief, but someone kept choking them. Suppressed cries have their own unique effect, chillingly penetrating and heart-rending. The present wailing, too, was of that kind. It could have shaken to the core even the most hard-hearted man.

Following the sound, the group reached a small chowk. It was a little open space where a number of lanes ended—or started—and which, on more normal days, functioned as a play area for the neighbourhood children. Any other day it would have been filled with colours and shouts, but today it was desolate—and silent. It seemed as though the noise of the approaching steps had reached the house of grief and the women's mouths had been clamped shut.

The policemen swiftly took position outside every house fronting the chowk. The officers gathered behind a pillar and began to argue about their next step. One thing was definite: the house in which the women had been wailing was right there somewhere—the sound had ceased the moment they had walked into the chowk. The officers—still huddling behind the pillar—strained their necks to look for that thin track of blood, but it was not easy. It was no longer just the rain. Here, every surrounding roof had drain spouts directly opening on to that little open space. The water that had collected on the roofs was pouring down on the paving stones and washing them clean.

Suddenly one of the jawans waved excitedly. He had been huddling against the door of a large haveli-type house. The little projection over the door had given him some shelter from the rain. And here he had noticed a red spot on the threshold. The projection overhead had protected it; still it had been washed out quite a bit. That's why it had taken the man some time to notice it, even though he had been standing right next to it. Some inspectors and policemen stepped out from where they had taken cover, then, still hugging the ground, they ran over to him.

As they bent down to examine that first spot of blood, they noticed other, still more faint, spots. Definitely, a wounded person had been taken to that house.

One officer softly knocked on the door. Inside there was total silence. He knocked a bit louder. No sound came from within the house. He stepped back and gestured to one of the sub-inspectors. The sub-inspector stepped forward and started hammering on the door with his fist. When still no sound came from inside, he gave the door several kicks. It was an old door and almost fell apart. Perhaps that's why a sound could now be heard from inside. Someone was approaching. The officers quickly took position on either side of the door. A couple of them pulled out their revolvers.

The steps came close, then stopped. Clearly someone was standing on the other side, trying to decide whether to open the door. Then the sound of the bolt being unlatched was heard and, with funereal silence, the door slowly opened.

An expressionless old face peered out. Looking at it one could have no idea of what might have happened in the house earlier.

'Everyone's gone deaf suddenly? We have been here ages—beating on the door and getting drenched.'

The speaker's angry words had no effect on the old man. His absolute silence even seemed belligerent. Some rain had splattered on his forehead, and water drops glistened on his white beard.

'Is some wounded person hiding inside?'

'No sir . . . there is no one.' His tone was so certain that even though everyone knew he was lying no one shouted at him.

'*Bade Miyan*, we're asking only to help the wounded man. You hand him over to us. We'll take him to the hospital in our van. He might be saved if he gets there in time. Who knows how long the curfew will last. If he doesn't get treated he might get worse.'

'You're the master, *huzur*. The house is open. You may look for yourself. There is no one inside.'

He gestured towards the inside of the house but didn't move aside. He stood blocking the doorway. No one knew what to do.

His utterly expressionless face and the persistent rain had combined to fill the atmosphere with mystery—as in a tale of magic.

Seeing everyone so nonplussed, the old man began to close the door. That movement broke the spell. One officer quickly inserted his cane between the two panels of the door. Another leaped forward and pushed the door open, sending the old man reeling back.

Immediately behind the door was a small room, after which was the *angan* (inner courtyard), surrounded by a veranda on all four sides. Then there were other rooms that opened facing the angan. In the veranda was a charpoy surrounding which stood several women, two or three young men, and a few children. On the bare charpoy lay the wounded man. Some blood had dripped through the webbing and spattered the floor below. Though the man's clothes were covered with blood, one could still see where the left side of his shirt stuck to the body some inches below the shoulder and looked darker and thicker. That's where the bullet had struck.

A sub-inspector ran his experienced eye over the inert figure and whispered into the ear of his senior officer, 'He is dead, sir.'

The officer looked around in alarm. No one had overheard. The people gathered around the charpoy still believed that the man was only wounded and had not died. Particularly the women. It is also possible that some of them may have realized the truth but had not been willing to accept it.

The women began their wailing again. Most of them had drawn their dupattas low over their foreheads to observe purdah and were expressing their grief in tight voices and incomprehensible words. Their bodies were swaying gently, and their movements and lamentation blended in a curious harmony. That harmony broke only if one of them suddenly cried more loudly than the others or if her body swayed more rapidly.

The officers looked at each other and came to a silent agreement. One of them ordered a subordinate, 'Take the man out on the charpoy itself. We'll surely find a doctor at the Colvin.'

Four or five constables swiftly moved forward and lifted the charpoy. But the men and women surrounding it remained where they were. They did not move, though the wailing stopped.

'You should give a hand, too. The sooner we get to the hospital the better.'

There was some stirring among the people standing around. A couple of men put their hands to the charpoy. Slowly its bearers began to move towards the door.

One woman suddenly remembered something. She hurriedly brought a bed cover and covered the wounded man with it. Outside it was raining again. The old man who had opened the door took the umbrella hanging from a peg in the veranda, half opened it over the face of the body, then closed it. He felt assured that the umbrella could protect the man from the rain.

The bearers had lifted the charpoy only waist-high. When they reached the front door, they stopped. The charpoy couldn't be carried out through the door as it was; it needed to be tilted to go through. The men at its foot stepped outside, then took hold of the charpoy. The people on one side stepped away. Now the people on three sides of it tilted the charpoy and started moving it through. But it kept getting stuck. Clearly a great deal more care and patience was needed. The charpoy was tilted more and more, until the body on it was about to roll off. A couple of jawans jumped forward and held it down. The officer who was supervising the whole thing from the back shouted in exasperation at the man who had shown impatience: 'Be careful there! The corpse could have fallen off.'

That word—'corpse'—shattered the atmosphere. The women suddenly stopped—frightened. The old man drew a loud breath and stopped, leaning with his full weight on his umbrella. Suddenly he had become so old that he needed to support himself.

Now, for the first time, the women began to wail as they normally do. Their voices, suppressed so far, began to rise and fall. Some began to beat their breast noisily. The thin veil of doubt that they had woven around themselves had now been ripped apart. When the wounded man had been brought in, he must have shown some signs of life. Gradually his body had become still. But the women had not been willing to accept that. The officer's words had forced them to face the fact for the first time.

A couple of women ran forward and, with outstretched arms, fell across the dead man. By then the charpoy had been brought outside. Half of it was under the overhang above the door while the other half was in the rain. Those who were holding its foot were fully exposed. When the two women threw themselves on the charpoy, it crashed to the ground. Now the remaining women also ran forward and surrounded the charpoy. Above was the pouring rain; below, the wailing women; and standing around them was a small crowd of silent, rain-drenched, devastated men.

Then some of the men stepped forward and slowly began to move the women away from the charpoy. Some of the women kept rushing back again and again to hold on to the corpse.

Finally, a couple of men used a bit of force and dragged them away.

Some of the jawans and the men from the house picked up the charpoy again. This time they placed it on their shoulders and, taking rapid steps, hurried to get out of the lane. About ten yards away was a sharp turn. First the charpoy disappeared, then slowly the small crowd trailing after it. Only the wailing of the women pursued them, but gradually they got out of its range too. If there had not been all the houses blocking the view, they would have seen that the women had gone back inside and only an old man still stood in the open door, oblivious to the rain, leaning on an umbrella. He should have closed the door but he had forgotten, or perhaps he was thinking that there was no longer any need to close it. Perhaps that's why he stood there, silent, at a loss.

2

Simultaneous with the curfew, a number of other things occurred on their own. For one, a certain part of the city was termed 'Pakistan' and the people living there were declared 'Pakistanis'. That was the area between Johnsonganj and Atala and between Khuldabad and Mutthiganj. A couple of times every year, the people of the rest of the city were bound to declare the people of that part to be 'Pakistanis'. For the past several years, whenever a curfew was declared in the city, it would actually be in that part alone. The city beyond that area would be happily lost in itself, oblivious to any incidents over there. The passengers getting down at Allahabad Junction on the Civil Lines side would have no sense at all of the fearful desolation prevailing on the chowk side. Life would go on merrily in the markets of Katra, Kydaganj and Civil Lines, while the people in the chowk and Mutthiganj would wait for the few precious hours when the curfew would be lifted and they could, sheep-like, pour out into the streets and experience some relief from their confinement.

15

It happened this time too. Curfew was imposed on the 'Pakistani' part of the city. Some streets ran right between Muslim and Hindu neighbourhoods. Life came to a standstill on the Muslim side; while on the Hindu side, it merely slowed down.

For Sayeeda, this was her first curfew. She had been visiting her village when a curfew was declared last June. But this time, when the curfew was clamped down, she was in the chowk near the clock tower, where she had gone with her younger daughter to get her some homoeopathic medicine. Her elder daughter had stayed behind at home with her grandmother. Since the day the little girl fell ill Sayeeda had been begging her mother-in-law to accompany her to the clinic, but the older woman had kept postponing it. Perhaps because of their work as bidi-makers: you could jeopardize your next meal if you wasted even a couple of hours on something else. Perhaps also because Sayeeda had two daughters, one after another, and the old woman was not much interested in daughters.

She simply told Sayeeda to give the girl some home remedy, and Sayeeda did. But this morning, when Sayeeda saw that the girl was in bad shape, she begged and cajoled her neighbour, Saiphunnisa, and got her to come with her. In return, she agreed to accompany Saiphunnisa to the bangle shop that the latter had wanted to go to for a long while.

The two had just stepped out of the clinic after getting the medicine when the curfew was announced.

But, in fact, there had been no actual announcement. It was Saiphunnisa's previous experience that told her that a curfew had been declared. The entire chowk was in turmoil. Store shutters were being pulled down helter-skelter, and their noise filled the air with a fear that was palpable. Children play with bricks by making them stand on their shorter edges in a line, then giving the first one a push. One after another all the bricks fall with a wave-like domino effect. In the same way now, clusters of people were fleeing and pushing others towards the chowk from the Nakkhas.

'Ya khuda . . . have mercy,' a muffled cry escaped from Saiphunnisa's lips and she grabbed Sayeeda's wrist. Sayeeda's mouth opened in surprise, but before any words could come out, Saiphunnisa had dragged her down the cloth market some twenty or thirty yards.

'What happened, sister?'

'Karphu . . . karphu . . . Ya khuda, get us home somehow.'

But every homeward step was an ordeal. Crowds kept rushing out from every direction. Shopkeepers were desperately gathering the goods they had spread out on the ground. Then there were the *ekkas*, rickshaws, bicycles and cars, jostling with each other to move forward. The broad street that on other days was sufficient for its traffic now seemed crowded like a narrow lane.

Saiphunnisa, pulling Sayeeda along by the hand, somehow managed to reach the fruit market. The pushcarts that usually crowded the open market were all gone. That their owners had fled with them either into various lanes or towards the clock tower was evident from all the mangoes, apples and oranges that lay scattered in the dirt and were being trampled underfoot by the people rushing headlong in desperation. Totally confused, Saiphunnisa ran into the fruit market, dashed across its open area, and was immediately lost in the labyrinthine lanes of Mirganj.

Mirganj's 'flesh market' was deathly silent. The prostitutes had slammed their doors shut. The spectators and pleasure-seekers who used to crowd the lanes were nowhere to be seen.

Every fourth or fifth house had a partially opened window from behind which peeped the face of some woman, her eyes eloquently expressing the anger and helplessness she felt. They, of course, had experienced several riots before. Each time during the curfew their condition would gradually deteriorate towards starvation; in some homes, they would be forced to subsist on boiled rice-water after just a couple of days.

Saiphunnisa had been in that area before. On a couple of earlier occasions she had come to its shops with her husband; each time she had peeked into the inner lanes and curiously surveyed the scene. But it was Sayeeda's first time; that's why she was feeling a strange mixture of guilt, excitement and shame. Without being told, she had realized what the place was. Meanwhile, Saiphunnisa rushed on, holding her by the wrist. The sudden silence and her own fear filled the lanes with some uncanny mystery. When some fleeing person would rush by them in similar desperation, she could feel the terror rise in her. Repeatedly losing themselves in that labyrinth, the two finally emerged again on G.T. Road, near the Gur Mandi.

By then the road was fairly empty of people. A police jeep sped by. Someone on it was using a megaphone to announce the curfew. He was appealing to the people to return immediately to their homes.

This sudden clamping down of a curfew was a terrible, new experience for Sayeeda. Tightly holding her child to her breast, she let herself be dragged along by Saiphunnisa. Saiphunnisa was more experienced and brave, and Sayeeda felt safe leaving herself in Saiphunnisa's hands. In fact, it had been only four years for Sayeeda in the city; she still felt like a stranger. Her own 'home' was near Pura Muphti and four years after marriage, she still pined for it. Her husband and his entire family made bidis. For a few months in the beginning, he sometimes took Sayeeda shopping or to a movie; but after that, Sayeeda would often need a companion to go to the market and only Saiphunnisa would come to her rescue. Saiphunnisa's husband was a chaprasi in the Geep factory, and received an assured amount of money every month. Saiphunnisa also made bidis, but only for a little extra income. Sayeeda's situation was different: making bidis was their only livelihood. The entire family had to toil every day for nearly fourteen hours before they could hope to have enough income for two square meals. After barely a couple of months of marriage and a few shopping trips and movies, Sayeeda had realized that it was imperative for her and her husband to join the other members of the family in their single, dark and dank room, to sit on the floor, bent over, making bidis and tying up the bundles, then fall asleep at night, confident that they had at least managed to feed the children.

Dashing headlong through unfamiliar alleys, desperately holding on to Saiphunnisa's wrist, Sayeeda was beginning to think that her flight would never end. But they did finally arrive in their own lane. It, too, was totally deserted. Nevertheless, Sayeeda immediately began to feel somewhat safe.

The doors were tightly shut; so were all the windows. Such silence. Such desolation. Sayeeda had never experienced anything like it. She was scared she may not recognize her home. But as their footsteps echoed in the lane, a few windows also rattled. As if someone opened a window for half a second, peeped out, then slammed it shut again. At each sound, Sayeeda's heart jumped with fright.

Saiphunnisa's house came first; Sayeeda's house was further down the lane. After Saiphunnisa jerked her wrist free and dashed into her own house, Sayeeda had to run the rest of the way alone. By the time she reached her door, she felt it had taken her ages to get past the remaining houses. She tried to knock softly, but when her hand touched the door, she realized that actually she was desperately beating on it.

The first sound she heard was her mother-in-law's cough. Then some masculine steps came close to the door and stopped. Sayeeda recognized them: it was her husband. Suddenly she felt an intense need to cry. As she had come closer to her house, some unfamiliar urge seemed to have gripped her, compelling her to cry. And the moment her husband opened the door she in fact started to cry. First in broken sobs, then quite loudly.

Sayeeda's mother-in-law came forward and took the sick child from her. The little girl looked much worse than she had in the morning. Gently caressing the child's head, the old woman, too, began to cry. For the first time, Sayeeda felt some maternal love directed towards herself and began to cry still more loudly.

'There, there . . . nothing happened . . . it will be all right. Allah shall take care of everything.'

When she heard these words, Sayeeda felt as if nothing had actually happened, that in fact everything would be all right. In any case, she didn't really know what had happened. She had only rushed home, past other desperately running people, through the terror of desolate lanes. She had only heard Saiphunnisa say that something called 'karphu' had been imposed, that it stopped people from stirring out of their homes. The next two days swiftly taught her what it actually meant to be unable to stir out of one's home.

3

At the beginning, the curfew was equally felt in all parts of the city, but soon it became less effective in the neighbourhoods which were not deemed 'Pakistani'. Hindus lived there and, as Hindus, obviously, they were the true lovers of the country. So it happened that they remained shut up in their homes only for the first few hours; then they unlocked their doors, threw open the windows and started looking around to see what was going on. The children, slipping away from their parents, ran outside and squatted on stoops and terraces. Every once in a while, the parents rushed out, grabbed the children by the ears, and dragged them howling and screaming inside. Though not for long. The moment they were free, the children ran out again. At intervals, police came by—in groups of two or three—scolded the children and sent them scampering back inside; then they themselves disappeared into the lanes, lazily sounding their staffs on the stoops.

The children grew bolder. They started their games—*gullidanda* to cricket—outside in the lanes. Some women came and stood at their doors and exchanged news. They had two main worries: that the children didn't run out of the lanes and into the streets in pursuit of their games, and that their husbands come home safely from their jobs. In most families, the bread-earners had not yet returned. Some even had children stuck at schools. With each passing hour, the women's anxiety increased.

This particular lane was a dense neighbourhood of closely constructed homes, except for a small expanse in the middle which lay empty. Someone had bought that plot years ago but never built anything on it. It had become the neighbourhood's garbage lot; also, for years, women of the neighbourhood, in moments of collective joy or sorrow, would gather there and talk. Today, too, some of them came there. In the homes where husbands and children had returned, the women gathered their loved ones inside, then hurried to watch the outside scene from windows and roofs. Other women who still had some member of the family missing gathered in that open space. Their voices were excited, but filled with anxiety.

Darkness was gradually spreading. It seemed the curfew was now well in place. The pace of people coming back slowed down. In fact, except for one or two men, only some children had managed to return. As they straggled back, a few women went indoors with them. The returnees brought with them plenty of rumours; each had something different to tell. 'Scores of dead Hindus are lying in the gutters.' 'The police have taken hundreds of corpses in trucks and dumped them into the Jamuna.'

This lane was almost identical to another not too far away in which the Muslims lived. Like it, it was filthy, poverty-ridden and stinking. The overflow from the latrines filled its gutter too. These things didn't matter much to its residents, but others coming from outside were obliged to cover their nose with a handkerchief. Nevertheless, this was a lane of Hindus, so the curfew did not make its residents absolute prisoners in their homes—it merely restricted them to their lane.

The arrival of Devi Lala in the lane was like comic relief. Like any other day, Devi Lala had gone out in the morning and, like any other day, was now staggering back home. What was different today was that he had come back a few hours before his regular time late at night. Usually, most of the residents would be sitting down to eat when Devi Lala's harsh, drunken voice would rise in the lane. But today he had returned early. And, unlike other days, he was neither warbling a song nor displaying the assurance that alcohol provides. In fact, he looked rather troubled. For one, he had not had enough to drink; for another, on the way back he had stumbled and fallen several times. There were scratches on his body, and the bottoms of his pyjamas dripped with filth.

Devi Lala was a 'blood-seller'. Every third or fourth day he would go to the Swarup Rani Hospital and sell some of his blood, returning home richer by some Rs 40 or 50. On the strength of that income he would go and get drunk on country liquor every evening. Today, however, he could only manage to sell his blood; he had not been able to get a drink. The curfew came down too fast. If he had known it, he would have first got a drink or two and only then entered the affected area. Now he was trapped in a maze of terrifying noises—of hurriedly pulled-down steel shutters; bewildered, stampeding people; the policemen's banging lathis. He could only blindly keep on running and when eventually he had to stop for breath, he found himself at the mouth of his own lane.

The moment they saw Devi Lala, some of the boys began to chant their daily chorus:

'Devi has a pair of caps,
Goats have two ears;
Devi Lala went to shit,
The Devil grabbed his rear.'

Despite the circumstances, some women began to giggle; a few shouted at the children to be quiet. Whether it was the terror-filled atmosphere or the utterly disarrayed sight of Devi Lala, today the children shut up. Unlike other days, they didn't prance around Devi Lala or raise their voices higher to make things worse for him. As for Devi Lala, not having had a drink, he felt as if his body was cracking apart; he was also having a great deal of trouble speaking. Then a woman shouted: '*Arrey*, Lala, did many people die in the riot?'

The question was addressed to Devi Lala, who immediately began to feel very special—he had come back so late in the curfew and had also wandered through so many affected areas. Narrowing his eyes in his peculiar manner, he mustered all his self-confidence and opened his mouth. The lack of a drink caused him to stammer, but he valiantly struggled to appear in control.

'Arrey, *chachi*, there are nothing but corpses in the city. I myself saw two trucks go by filled with corpses . . . the police were taking them away to throw them in the Jamuna. *Musallas* [pejorative abbreviation of Mussulman] are running all over the place . . . flashing their knives and daggers. Poor Hindus . . . they have no one to protect them.'

'*Hey bhagwan* . . . what will happen to those who haven't come back yet?'

The faces of the women whose husbands or children had not returned home paled. A few even started to wail softly. But those whose family members were safe at home were eager to satisfy their curiosity.

'So, Lala, the Muslims are roaming everywhere with knives despite the police?'

'Roaming? They're knifing everyone. Some I saw with my own eyes. Helpless Hindus are dropping like flies. It doesn't take these Musallas long to kill someone. What can the police do to them? So many corpses . . . I just barely avoided stepping on several myself!'

Devi Lala went on yapping. Not having had a drink frequently made him lose his confidence, but the urgent curiosity on the faces of his listeners immediately gave him the necessary boost to go on. He continued to talk, and troubled, excited faces kept listening to him. He would stop only when some other male resident of the lane returned all aflutter—dripping wet, his trousers or pyjamas filthy with mud. The eager crowd would immediately surround him. The newcomer would excitedly tell them some new 'facts' and stand around enjoying their looks of disbelief until his wife or children would forcibly drag him home.

Seven or eight police and PAC jawans—sounding their staffs on the paving stones—stepped out into the lane. The swarm of listeners scattered in panic. Some of the jawans found that amusing; they hit their staffs on the ground harder and, uttering loud abuses, pretended to run in pursuit. The fleeing people ran harder, splashing through the muck and shit that had overflowed from the gutter, and paused only when they were safely behind bolted doors.

Once they got inside, the children pressed their noses against the windows and fixed their eyes on the policemen outside. The women glued themselves to the cracks in the front doors. The men, however, burdened with their sense of being men, couldn't overtly display their curiosity. So they sat in clammy hot rooms under ceiling fans and scratched their badly itching bodies. The rain had stopped long ago, and once again it was suffocatingly damp and hot.

The policemen sat down on a terrace; a few of them even stretched out on its floor. Devi Lala, in his blind dash, had taken shelter behind a heap of garbage. Earlier in the day, he had received a few blows on his legs and back from police sticks; that's why he had panicked. But he couldn't suffer the awful stench of the garbage for long; eventually he mustered some courage and peeped out. He noticed that among the men on the terrace there was also a constable from the local *chowki*, whom he knew only as 'Mishra' and with whom he'd even had a few drinks in the past. Devi Lala's courage returned; he stood up, almost stumbling over the garbage heap.

'Jai Hind, Panditji. I was scared for nothing.'

'Who's that? Devi Lala? Jai Hind, Jai Hind. Where've you been hiding? What kind of a *mohalla is* this, anyway? *Sasur!* We can all die here of thirst. Haven't had a drop of water since noon. Come on, *bhai,* get us some tea or something.'

Devi Lala dashed over to a house and started beating upon its door.

'Who's there?' a female voice asked from inside. 'What do you want? There is no man at home.'

'How can that be? Arrey, I myself saw Ramsukh Compositor go in. Bhai, I'm Devi Lala. Darogaji is standing here outside. Open the door, he needs water.'

Ramsukh Compositor didn't stir forth, but his wife, reassured by Devi Lala's voice, partially opened the door.

Devi Lala was bursting with excitement—after all, he was in the company of policemen armed with guns and lathis. Loudly he called out to Ramsukh Compositor to come out and, when Ramsukh's wife again told him in a beseeching voice that her husband was not home, he flatly refused to believe her. The matter was finally settled when Ramsukh's wife agreed to make piping hot tea for everyone.

By the time the tea came, several windows had opened, partly or fully. A few children even felt bold enough to step outdoors, but the jawans shouted them back in. However, when the tea had to be served, Devi Lala asked Ramsukh's two sons to come out and help.

Seeing them, a few other neighbourhood boys also ventured out. At first the policemen scolded them half-heartedly, then got too busy with the tea. The boys at first audaciously stood at their front doors, then gradually stepped down into the lane. In no time at all, a small crowd of them collected around the police party. They longingly stared at the assortment of weapons and whispered to each other the names. Every so often, a policeman would snap at them or bang his lathi on the floor to shoo them away. The children would scamper away, but return in no time. Soon they started a chorus:

'Hindu-pulis bhai-bhai
Katua kaum kahan-se ai'
'The Hindus and the police are like brothers.
Where did these Katua people come from?'
[Katua kaum, another pejorative term for the Muslims. The words roughly mean, the trimmed people, or the circumcised people.]

The policemen laughed—a few jokingly cursed the children—then everyone went back to his tea. Devi Lala hurried off to arrange for their meal. The curfew was a frequent affair, and the policemen were accustomed to having an evening meal either in this lane or the one next to it. After enjoying the food and spending some time pleasantly joking with their hosts, they would amble off to the 'Pakistani' lanes to impose the real curfew.

There was no home in the lane that could provide adequate food for the entire police party. But Devi Lala knew everything about everyone. He had one family prepare puris, asked another to make the potato curry, then bullied a few others into dishing out assorted pickles and chutneys.

By the time the policemen sat down to eat, a fair number of men, having gained courage, had gathered around them. They were all Hindus; naturally, they were most concerned about the state of the nation. Some of them recognized a few of the jawans; others made new friends and excitedly began to tell them the 'secret' news only they knew. One claimed that there was a certain man in the 'Pakistani' lane who had a transmitter in his house and was using it to send the latest news abroad— how else could the BBC report in its evening bulletin a riot that had occurred only that afternoon? Some of his obviously envious neighbours wanted to know just when he listened to the BBC, but others promptly believed him. Other men described certain houses in the 'Pakistani' lane in which, according to them, arms had been stored. Each man gave different details according to his own general knowledge. Most of them had only learned about revolvers and bombs from the usual films and newspapers; they only reported caches of the same. A few better-informed men, however, reported even Sten

28

guns. The police took note of all the reports. In every riot, the police always made sure to teach the 'Pakistanis' a lesson; this time, too, these special reports were going to come in handy for that purpose.

When the meal was finished, the jawans washed their hands and rinsed their mouths leaning over the gutter. Then, after standing around for a little while more, relaxed and picking their teeth, they strolled off to teach the 'Pakistanis' a lesson.

By now it was quite late. Normally the lane would be fast asleep by this time, but tonight there were still plenty of people out—scattered in small groups on stoops and terraces. However, unlike other nights, no one had brought out his charpoy to sleep over the gutter. Tonight, they all had to sleep indoors—despite the fact that it was a 'Hindu' lane and that the curfew only actually required them not to go out into the main street. But even the thought of going inside—into the stifling heat—was unbearable. So the people lingered outside and continued to gossip. They were confident that they were entirely safe where they were. The only worried people were those who earned their wages daily; they knew that the longer the curfew extended, the less food there would be on their plates. During the past few years, the 'rulers' of the city had always delayed lifting the curfew until they were convinced that the citizens had been fully taught a lesson. For the daily-wagers, however, just a couple of days of curfew would be enough to make them cry.

Suddenly, at one end of the lane, it sounded as if some stones hit a door. The people jumped and ran for shelter. Several stumbled and fell. Some women began to shriek. Scrambling to protect their children, the mothers themselves almost fell down. But the panic lasted only a few moments. People quickly realized that no one had attacked them, that in fact some boys huddling at that end of the lane had thrown a few bricks at Yusuf Tailor's door.

Yusuf Tailor was the only Muslim in the lane. At the time of Partition, his brothers had migrated to Pakistan; only he had stayed behind. Every time there was a riot, his wife would start cursing him for his now-ancient folly, and he would resolve to sell his house and move to some safer location. Then—when peace had returned—he would go searching for a house everywhere, only to resume his work after a couple of days, silently bent over some piece of cloth. The riot would make only one change in his family's life: they would all become prisoners in their home. They would seal up the house from inside, piling planks and charpoys against the front door, and huddle in the rooms—dead silent.

Yusuf Tailor had nine children. Six were girls, each of a different age. And each was 'involved' with some boy or the other as suited her age. These were like all the other local involvements, which would begin when a pair started going to school and end the moment one of the pair got married. It never happened that the boy and the girl who secretly threw glances at each other or exchanged love notes between pages of books and notebooks actually got married to each other. It was not likely to happen in the future either. That's why Yusuf Tailor's daughters, while going to school or while standing in their doorway or at the upstairs window, would disinterestedly look at the boys passing and smile or hurry by them in the street with downcast eyes. That evening, too, if only to relieve the fatigue caused by the curfew one or another of the girls came and stood at the upstairs window, to move away with a smile at the whistles and cracks of the boys sitting on the opposite stoop.

Judged by the standards of the lane, Yusuf Tailor's ancestral house was fairly big. There were two rooms downstairs, with an angan and a kitchen; upstairs, there was only one room and an open roof. Only the parapet walls were unusually high—Yusuf had them raised out of concern for his six daughters and the frequent riots.

As in other curfews, the house was filled with terror and silence. Yusuf and his wife had bolted the front door and piled against it all the planks and charpoys they could find. He had managed to close his shop and got home with great difficulty after the curfew had been announced. After barricading the door, he had collapsed face down on his bed, while his wife padded around cursing him in a low voice. For a while, his children hid in corners, scared to death. Then, as it grew dark, the older girls briefly sneaked upstairs, taking turns. The mother started the evening meal and ordered a couple of them to give her a hand in the kitchen. The father remained where he lay, and ground his teeth and cursed his sons whenever any made the slightest noise.

When the food was ready, the entire family sat down together. Yusuf's wife served, while Yusuf, his head lowered as usual, concentrated on eating. The children—frightened by Yusuf's demeanour—also ate in utter silence. Meanwhile, the boys sitting outside in the lane ran out of patience. First they tossed a pebble or two at the upstairs window; then, when none of the girls made an appearance, they got exasperated and threw a couple of bricks at Yusuf's door.

The crash of the bricks and the noise of the mad scramble outside struck unimaginable terror in the hearts of Yusuf's family. The younger children began to howl. The hands of the older children stopped in mid-air, their frightened eyes fixed on the front door. Yusuf too numbly stared. The door was well fortified, but still it was very old. How long would it last under pressure from outside? Leaping up, he and his wife rushed around and found some more heavy things to pile against the door.

The panic outside had been momentary. People had quickly realized that there had been no attack from outside, that in fact it was some of the local boys who had thrown a couple of bricks at Yusuf Tailor's door. They loudly cursed them. Even the men who had talked of 'Pakistani transmitters' and 'caches of weapons' couldn't imagine how there could be an attack on a Muslim's house in their own lane. So many of them now began to shout at the culprits that they finally slunk off to hide their shame.

The residents of the lane realized that in all the hullabaloo they had completely forgotten that one house. Now they gathered before it. A few of them called out loudly to Yusuf to open the door. But not the slightest sound came from inside.

'It's only the first day; he won't open the door,' someone remarked.

That was true. In previous curfews, Yusuf's door had never opened on the first few days.

'Don't worry, Yusuf Bhai; we're here with you,' Devi Lala somehow managed to call out, his tongue parched for a drop of alcohol. The boys promptly turned his words into a slogan, and started a new chant:

'Yusuf, tum sangharsh karo; hum tumhare sath hain.'

'Yusuf, start the struggle; We stand by your side.'

There had been elections quite recently and the popular political slogan was still on the boys' lips. Their elders again tried to scold them, but this time had no success. Finally everyone wandered away.

After a while, the upstairs window reopened and the boys gradually drifted back and settled on the stoop across the lane.

4

It was the second day of the curfew and Sayeeda's little girl was in very bad shape.

The high heat of August had turned their closed room into a stinking hell, filled with the stench of several sweating bodies and the two littlest children's bowel movements. Ten people were confined to a space defined by a room thirteen by eight feet, and a veranda eight by five feet. The adults included Sayeeda, her husband, her in-laws, her elder sister-in-law, and her two young brothers-in-law; her seven-year-old nephew and her two daughters were the three children.

When Sayeeda had first arrived after her marriage, she had found it very hard to adjust to a whole lot of things. The neighbourhood was primarily Muslim, and, like most Muslim neighbourhoods, it simmered with poverty, ignorance and filth. Sayeeda had a hard time convincing herself that one small room was all there was to her new home; and that it was in that room, in the presence of several adults, that she would have to start her married life. In the beginning she frequently felt numb, so impossible did her situation seem. That one-room house had a small veranda at the back, right next to which was a tiny latrine that was never quite clean. A peculiarly foul smell always came from it. It took Sayeeda several months to reconcile herself to living with that sickening smell.

It was in that veranda that Sayeeda had enjoyed the initial pleasures of marital life. Except for the first night—when her in-laws took the rest of the family with them to sleep outside in the lane, over the gutter—one or another of the adults had always slept in that room. Sometimes the entire family slept there. Usually her husband would spread his bedding on the floor in the back veranda and lie there impatiently waiting for her. Whenever Sayeeda was late, he would start coughing in a ridiculous manner. Hearing the sound, Sayeeda's body would stiffen like wood. She always felt very angry at his shameless behaviour. But then she would get up and, somehow stepping over the sleeping bodies sprawled on the floor, go and lie down beside him—no longer angry.

It was the second day of the curfew, and, except for Sayeeda, the rest of family knew that there was not going to be any relief for a few more days.

Confined to the house, Sayeeda was faced with two serious problems. One was her little girl's condition. It had so deteriorated that Sayeeda's more experienced mother-in-law was beginning to believe that the girl was not likely to survive. The old woman had had eleven children, seven of whom were already dead. She was so accustomed to seeing children die that now she could sense any sick child's imminent death.

Sayeeda's second problem was of a peculiar nature. She had come to the city from a place where just the thought of it was laughable. There she would rise, right at dawn, and—an aluminium *lota* in hand, and accompanied by a sister or some neighbourhood girl—walk out far into the fields. Except for a couple of zamindars, no one in her village had a latrine in his house. The women went out into the fields in the twilight hours of dawn and dusk. After harvest, when the fields didn't provide enough cover, they would squat behind some bush or beside the raised boundary lines of the fields. This routine was broken only when it rained or when someone came down with diarrhoea.

Sayeeda's mother-in-law had told her on the very first day what she was expected to do in the city. They themselves had come from the village, and Sayeeda's mother-in-law knew what a village woman coming to live in the city had to face. That first evening, when Sayeeda stepped into the latrine, she almost collapsed trying not to throw up. Her eyes started to water, and a bilious drool oozed out of the corners of her clenched lips and spotted her clothes. The latrine was only six feet by three and had a raised 'seat'; its roof was so low that it was almost impossible to stand in it. This dark damp place was always filled with a sharp odour that would burst through the whole house the moment someone opened its door. In fact, even with the door closed, that awful smell was faintly present everywhere. To live with it one had to get accustomed to it, and that took Sayeeda several months.

The latrine was cleaned once a day. In the beginning, Sayeeda tried to be smart. The sweeper came around seven or seven-thirty in the morning. He would come and make a noise on the doorsteps with his tool—that announced his arrival. Immediately, Sayeeda's mother-in-law or someone else would check to make sure that no one was in the latrine, then inform the sweeper. In order to do his job, the sweeper had to go to the back where the lower part of the latrine had an opening—

about one foot square—covered with a piece of tin hanging from a couple of nails. The tin was so time-worn and battered that the sweeper daily expected to find it fallen to the ground. It took Sayeeda only a few days to discover this routine. She started waiting for the sweeper's arrival; the moment he was done, she would rush into the latrine. The trouble was that in the village she had got into the habit of going to the toilet very early. To wait now till 7 a.m. or later was excruciating. She often had to contort her body in all sorts of ways to control herself.

It didn't take long for Sayeeda's mother-in-law to catch on to her. She was incensed that this girl, who had not been with them for very long, considered herself superior to the rest of the family. One morning, she told Sayeeda off in the foulest terms. Sayeeda felt so ashamed and hurt that she went and hid in a corner for quite some time. But in a few days, the mother-in-law—who was also Sayeeda's aunt—began to feel sorry for her. She saw a few times how nauseated Sayeeda looked as she staggered out after using the latrine.

Not far from their house, where the lane ended, lay an empty plot of land. Someone had bought it to build a house and even had the foundations laid, but then had left it unused. Behind it was the drainage ditch that ran parallel to the lane quite a way, then continued northwards. During the day, that was where all the children hung around, played games and made a ruckus. Sayeeda's mother-in-law started taking her there in the morning. Sometimes the two would squat in a corner of that empty plot, at other times they would move to the edge of the drain ditch. To get to the ditch one had to go down a bit of a slope, and the two women had to hold each other's arm to support each other. Still the older woman stumbled a couple of times and hurt her ankles; each time she cursed Sayeeda until she had her in tears. The bigger problem was that the two had to get up extremely early—when every night they could never go to sleep before 11 p.m. In fact, Sayeeda had to stay awake longer for the sake of her husband. Getting up that early, therefore, left the two nodding all day long.

After about a week, the mother-in-law had had it, but she did give Sayeeda permission to go by herself. The mere thought of that latrine in the back was so nauseating to Sayeeda that every day she got up at an ungodly hour no matter what. If some night her husband kept her awake too late, she would just lie there the remaining few hours, scared that she might fall asleep and the sun would come up. She would lie there, half awake, half asleep, and frequently sit up to peer at her husband's wristwatch to see how much time had passed. After such nights, she further had to suffer her mother-in-law's curses all day long.

By the end of the second day of the curfew, the bubbling latrine and the steaming heat had turned Sayeeda's home into a little hell, and its residents were beginning to collapse under its miasmic air. In the morning, Sayeeda had opened the door to go into the latrine but had reeled back, desperately struggling to suppress her nausea. The whole day went by, but she didn't use the place even once. She stopped eating; out of her fear, she did not even take any tea that morning.

Sayeeda's daughter had lain all day long in her grandmother's lap. Three days of dysentery had devastated the poor two-year-old. Today, since noon, she had been vomiting too—an obvious victim of cholera. But only her mother and grandmother were concerned about her. The father and the grandfather squatted in another corner of the gloom-filled room and were so lost in their bidi-making that anyone coming in from outside would have mistaken them for ghosts. Their naked torsos were sticky with sweat as their busy hands flew back and forth, phantom-like, over the small piles of bidi leaves, tobacco and thread. In the opposite corner, Sayeeda's two brothers-in-law and her nephew were listlessly playing carom. That was the only means of entertainment in the house, and the boys were getting bored with it, for they had been at it most of the day. They would play a few games, then quarrel and stop, only to start again after a while. Today their neglect of work didn't bring them kicks and curses because there weren't enough tobacco and leaves for everyone in the house. Only Sayeeda's sister-in-law was moving around, trying somehow to prepare some food for the family.

Sayeeda had brought home only two days' medicine, but in all the confusion and worry she had given it all to the baby in just twenty-four hours. By noon, there was none left. She had been casting scared glances at her husband; a few times—disregarding the respect she owed her father-in-law—she had even addressed her husband directly and begged him to get some more medicine. But the two men kept on working in their silent, stolid fashion.

Her husband had had a nasty experience that morning when he had agreed to fetch some water from the public tap; he was in no mood to listen to another such request. They had a tap in the house, but it let out only a faint drip of water and that too for only an hour or so mornings and evenings; their remaining need had to be met from the public tap at the entrance to the lane. Twice a day there was a mad scene out there when the neighbourhood women jostled and quarrelled as they tried to get whatever little water they could. Most of the houses in that lane had no more than one tap, which couldn't supply enough water even in the cold days of winter. Now, of course, it was hellishly hot and people could feel thorns in their throats. That's why that morning Sayeeda's husband, entreated by his mother, decided to take the risk of stepping out. Not a drop of water had come into the house from outside since the time the curfew was announced. What had dripped—as usual—from the tap in the house had been used. By dawn there was hardly more than a bucket left. So, when his mother begged him, Sayeeda's husband had picked up the buckets and stepped out into the cool twilight of the lane.

After more than twelve hours of confinement, the openness of the lane was delightfully soothing. The sun had not yet come out and a refreshing cool breeze blew. The lane was dead silent. The cots that used to line it end to end every night were nowhere to be seen. The familiar narrow lane seemed wide and open. The only living beings were some stray dogs. Even the cows that used to meander through the lane chewing cud, seemed to have been affected by the curfew and disappeared.

With a bucket in each hand, Sayeeda's husband took a few scared steps. The public tap was about a hundred yards away, but soon he could hear it. The tap was open and—it being quite early in the morning—running at full blast. The splash of the water on the ground could be heard even at a distance. No one, as usual, had bothered to shut the tap yesterday, and, equally as usual, water was pouring out of it at dawn. The only difference was that normally, even that early, there would be a few women at the tap, while today it seemed totally abandoned.

After a few more steps, his fear began to leave him. He even started to enjoy himself. The tiring night had left his body fatigued; now the gentle morning breeze freshened him. Softly he began humming a song. By the time he arrived at the tap he was so oblivious that he didn't notice how loud his song had become. Before placing a bucket under the tap, he cupped his hands under the cold jet and washed his face and arms. The water was coming out with such force that, despite his efforts, his lungi and vest were drenched. The water felt cold and its touch made him shiver with pleasure.

Whether it was due to his loud singing or their own desire to have a wash, there suddenly appeared two police jawans, yawning, still half asleep. He became aware of them only when they started cursing and lashing at him with their canes. 'Mother f . . . ! Bastard! What the f . . . are you doing here? Getting your mother f . . . ed?' They kept hitting him on his legs and hips.

His second bucket was barely half filled. He stumbled and almost fell down but, quickly recovering, he picked up the buckets and ran homeward. The jawans saw no purpose in running after him—perhaps they were too tired after being on duty all night. One of them cupped a hand under the tap and began to drink; the other stood by, shouting foul abuses at the fleeing man.

He stumbled several times and the water in his buckets kept splashing, but the fleeing man didn't slow down. He felt sure that the two messengers of death were still in hot pursuit. When he finally entered his house, there were barely four bowls of water left in the two buckets. That's why, despite Sayeeda's repeated—silent, as well as vocal—requests, he had felt no urge to go out for the child's medicine. He had kept his head bowed and continued with his work.

Frustrated, Sayeeda stopped saying anything to him. Whenever the child threw up or defecated in her grandmother's lap, Sayeeda would get up and, with a most miserly use of water, clean up the mess. Sayeeda's mother-in-law had seen several of her own children die; it wasn't difficult for her to realize that the little girl was nearing her end. But for Sayeeda it was her first experience as a mother.

After coming to the city, Sayeeda had seen several movies. Often the women in them sang songs about their deceased children or appeared to be lost in the memory of their innocent little pranks. Sayeeda tried to recall some little prank of her baby, but couldn't. What came to her mind was such a confusion of hunger, a running nose and filth that it didn't stir in her the kind of tender maternal love shown in the movies. She kept remembering that her breasts had not filled up with milk when the baby was born. Almost up to the time of birth, Sayeeda's first daughter—barely a year old—had continued to tug and pull at her nipples, and the grandmother had to scold and threaten her to stop her. Afterwards, Sayeeda had a hungry baby nipping at her breasts, and a little older child who whined and cried all the time. She couldn't understand why milk had not come into her breasts. Poverty and hard labour had broken her body and didn't let her become a complete mother. Often she would leave the two girls side by side on the floor and get busy with housework. The girls would howl and cry until they were out of breath. Meanwhile, the other members of the family—their heads bowed—would continue with their bidi-making. They were so accustomed to crying children, they never felt any need to stop and pay attention to them.

Today that same little girl was dying. Every atom in Sayeeda's body had become a mother and was crying out: her pitifully helpless daughter was dying before her eyes, but she could do nothing about it. Sayeeda's husband—bent over his bidis and showing no emotion—seemed to her like some cruel monster. She wanted to scream and scratch her husband's heartless chest till it bled.

Just as the dark silent surface of a lake is shattered when a stone is flung into it, the silence of that oppressive room too was shattered by Sayeeda's sudden shriek. The air in the room visibly trembled for a few moments. When the baby's breathing had become infrequent and she had started to blink her eyes much too often, the grandmother had realized that her time had come. But that realization came to Sayeeda only when she bent down to wipe the mix of vomit and drool from the baby's mouth and saw that her tiny little pupils had turned upwards and no longer moved. She felt the stab of an unspeakable pain and shrieked.

Death was something familiar—and easier—for Sayeeda's husband. Every year there was a death in the house or in the immediate neighbourhood. And usually it was some child. But God knows what it was about his own child's death that, despite all the pretence of indifference, he was shaken to the core by Sayeeda's first shriek. In two years he had probably cuddled his daughter like a father scarcely more than five or six times; yet now when she was suddenly no more, he sat numb, staring into empty space. The presence of his parents prevented him from crying. Meanwhile, Sayeeda, tears pouring from her eyes, was struggling to beat her head against the floor. The other women held her tight in their arms, but every so often she still managed to hit her head against the wall or the floor. For a brief moment, her husband felt a desire to go over to her and comfort her. Then he got up and, moving to the veranda in the back, began to cry himself. Perhaps it was his sense of guilt at being unable to do anything for his child that impelled his tears now.

5

The girl must have been about fifteen. My readers will not gain anything if I tell them her name. Names are tied to religion and in this great 'World Teacher' country of ours, religion can sometimes bring much satisfaction to the human self, but at other times it can cause severe suffering. For example, if this girl turns out to be a Hindu, she might cause Hindu stalwarts to drown themselves in shame; and if she happens to be a Muslim, she could put Islam in danger. That's why, dear readers, it's better that we regard her as neither Hindu nor Muslim, and think of her plight as simply that of an individual.

The girl, like the majority of girls in this land, was cursed to live with ignorance, poverty and dreams. Hindi films and 'Ranu's' romances had started to give shape to her innate feelings, and now she constantly dreamed about princes—who were never going to appear in her life. In the lane where this girl lived, human excrement bubbled in gutters that were cleaned only when some high official or minister happened to come by for 'inspection'. The girl's elder sister also used to dream of princes in long limousines, but last year she ran away with a boy from their lane. Luckily, within just three days, her father and brothers caught up with her on a railway platform in Bombay. Within a fortnight they had her married to a lineman whose first wife had died the previous year leaving behind three little children. That was bound to happen to this girl, too. And yet, because of her age, she now went about constantly humming some song.

The girl was returning home from school in the afternoon, as on any other day. She was in Class XI and her school was about three kilometres away from her home. It started at seven every morning. Because it had two shifts of classes, its time schedule never changed, no matter what the season. Every morning, the girl had to leave her house at 6 a.m. That wasn't so bad in the warm months, but in winter it was rather hard. She would often miss her first class. Lately, however, she had been leaving home punctually at 5.45 a.m.! The reason for it was not a sudden interest in studies—it was something else.

A little further down the lane lived a boy. He was a few years older than she was, and something of a dandy. The girl and the boy had lived for years in the same lane and hardly paid any attention to each other. But in the past few weeks they had been showing a great deal of interest in one another. What had happened was this. After the boy had passed his 'Inter' examination, his father advised him to find a job. The boy insisted on going on to do a BA, so the father slapped him around. The boy refused to eat for two days. The father explained to him the ratio of his own salary to the country's rate of inflation. The boy ran away from home. After a week or so, the father put an ad in a local newspaper. Under the boy's picture it said: 'Mother seriously ill. Come back.' The boy came back.

The father again gave him a thrashing. This time the boy didn't run away—he quietly started looking for a job. Somehow he turned out to be more fortunate than the rest of his generation. Without anyone's recommendation—and by giving a bribe of only Rs 2000 he got the job as a timekeeper at one of the factories in Naini. To put together the money, his father had to borrow from several colleagues at the office; now the boy, starting with his first salary, was struggling to pay them back.

The boy and his job were the reasons why the girl had started going to school every morning promptly at 5.45 a.m. The boy had to be at his factory by 8.00 a.m.; so he always left home at 6.00 a.m. It was almost a kilometre from his house to the bus stop. That was also the road the girl took to go to her school. One morning, following the same path, their eyes—as the idiom goes—'bumped into each other'. Not very many people were about at that hour; only once in a while would someone come along and hurry by. It was the ideal time for any two pairs of eyes to bump into each other.

At first the girl didn't notice anything. Then suddenly one day she became aware that the boy walking ahead of her was taking very short steps—as if he wanted to let her come abreast of him. The girl didn't know what to do: should she walk faster or slow down? By the time she came parallel to the boy, her body was shivering—her temples were hot with excitement. She slowed down. He slowed down further. The girl realized the inevitable. She, in fact, wanted it. The distance between them lessened. Then all her reluctance to get up so early disappeared, and the two started walking that one-kilometre stretch together every morning.

In that companionship of just half an hour every day, the two began to have dreams. She would frequently smile for no reason at all; he started carrying a comb in his hip pocket. The boy was getting a monthly salary of Rs 490. He would take out a hundred or so for buses and rickshaws; the rest he always put, like a good son, into his mother's hands on the first of the month. The hundred was his 'pocket money'. As a consequence of the new friendship, he had to cut into it. Last month, he treated the girl to a movie, gave her a fountain pen, and twice took her to a restaurant for a cup of tea. This month, he gave his mother a hundred rupees less—he told her it somehow fell out of his pocket. He wanted to give the girl a shawl as a present. He decided he would tell his mother some lie or other every month until he had saved enough for the gift, in time for winter. He had already told the girl about the shawl.

It was going to be the girl's first shawl ever. She could already feel its pleasing weight over her breasts and began to smile more frequently. She quietly got hold of a couple of pullovers that were no longer of any use to any member of her family and unravelled them; then she started knitting the wool into a sweater for the boy. She, of course, could not let her mother know about it and did it all secretly. At the end of every winter her mother would collect all the torn and worn-out sweaters in a big wicker basket; then, a couple of months before the following winter, she would combine all the usable wool from a couple of sweaters and knit a new one from it. Every pullover or sweater in that family would go through this process so many times that any 'new' sweater would start fraying after just a few weeks of use, and most likely be in tatters by the time winter ended. The girl quietly took what she needed from that basket and left it with a girl friend. She would collect the knitting from her friend on the way to school, work on it during the day, then leave it with her again while coming back. Her life—a confusion of poverty and romance— would have gone on like that for two or three years—until she either eloped with the boy or got married elsewhere—had not the curfew brutally rocked her world like an earthquake.

For almost a week the city's 'temperature' had been rising. The girl's parents were experienced. They knew the rising 'heat' would soon pounce upon the city in the form of a riot and that the city would suffer another curfew. Already the previous night the mother had told the girl, 'Don't go to school tomorrow.' But the school was tremendously important in the girl's life. The fact was that she had to spend all her time after school doing things at home. Her mother sewed petticoats for a dealer. When the girl returned home, her mother would sit down with her sewing—she could earn as much as Rs 10 every day. Meanwhile the girl would look after her younger brothers and sisters and also do the cooking and cleaning. Late at night, after all the work was done, she would sit down to study. Not that she could do anything more than just struggle to remain awake. When exams approached, her mother would let her have a bit more time. That was her unchanging, tiresome routine. The only break came in the morning when she went to school—she did not want to give up those sweet moments, no matter what. And so, despite her mother's admonition, she quietly got ready in the morning and set out for school without arousing anyone's suspicion.

But the boy had not come that day. The girl felt quite frustrated. She thought perhaps she was late and hurried on to the main road where the boy would catch his bus. There was less than a third of the normal number of people at the stop. Apparently many of them thought it better to stay home that day. The girl waited. The bus came and left. The boy turned out

47

to be a coward. He couldn't untie himself from the *anchal* of his mother's sari. The girl, mortified and angry, cursed his cowardice and turned around. But did she want to go back home to be further humiliated by her mother? She turned around again and set off for school.

Very few girls and teachers had come that day. As a result, there were no classes. The girls hung around the classrooms and had a boisterous time. The teachers sat in the principal's office and gossiped over many cups of tea.

Several times the girl thought of returning home, but the fear of her mother's anger and her own chagrin stopped her. Instead, she sat in the school compound and conversed with her girl friend. In truth, she listened more than she talked.

Suddenly the teachers burst out of the principal's office and ran in panic towards the gates. As they ran they shouted to any girl they encountered to hurry home immediately. Then a chaprasi came running towards the grounds, wildly waving his arms, and hollered to the girls, 'Run home!'

Girls rushed out from everywhere like cattle. Only when they reached the gates did most of them learn that there had been a riot in the city and a curfew had been declared.

The girl's home was in a lane where a curfew was imposed every year or two, but this was her first experience of finding herself running down a main street during a curfew. She ran blindly. The shops were being closed in a frenzy, and the loud bangs of their shutters were strangely terrifying. Any other day, even the thought of seeing countless bicycles and pedestrians dashing in confusion and heedless haste—stumbling, falling, colliding with each other—would have made her burst into laughter; but today, herself a part of that mad dash, she could barely keep her eyes free of tears.

It was the third lane off G.T. Road where the girl would turn to head home. Today, confused and frightened, she was dragged along into a different lane by some people who came rushing from behind. At first, she was part of a crowd, then suddenly, as if by magic, the crowd vanished, and the girl found herself in a lane that looked utterly desolate and strange. The houses had such an eerie look—their doors and windows were like tightly clenched jaws—she couldn't be sure if anyone lived in them. She began to shiver in terror. (The girl had in fact passed through that lane endless times. God knows why the same lane seemed totally unfamiliar today.)

She stopped and, taking cover in a doorway, desperately looked around for some sign of life. After a few minutes it became clear that the houses around her were not as deserted as they had seemed. Behind every little slit in every door and window were faces glued to them. When the shutters on any window would briefly part, she could see terrified eyes peering out. But then would come a fresh, muffled roar from G.T. Road, and all the telltale openings would suddenly vanish. At every little sound the girl's head would jerk up and she would nervously look around like a hunted deer.

The tough arms that brutally snatched the girl appeared from nowhere—she only heard the grating noise of the steel shutters behind her being raised. Before she could recover, six rough, male arms had pulled her into a small, narrow room that housed a milling machine. As she was dragged in, the girl's head struck hard against the shutters. The blow and the sudden attack stunned her. She wanted to scream but couldn't. Then the shutters were pulled down again, and she was flung upon a battered charpoy grimy with layers of flour.

'Bhaiya . . . I'm your sister . . . let me go!'

That was all the girl was able to say. It made the three men giggle. One of them picked up the dagger-like tool they used to cut open sacks of grain and moved to the head of the charpoy. The girl tried to say something, but . . . 'Shut up, *sali*. We f . . . sisters.'

The girl shut up. What she next experienced was obscene and terrifying. She felt as if a hot rod was pushed into her body. A wave of pain rose from the soles of her feet and went to the top of her head, leaving her body wracked. When an animal is slaughtered it makes a terrible gurgling sound—something of the same nature escaped the girl's lips. She struggled to get up, but only bruised herself more against the sides of the charpoy. Her crazily open eyes remained fixed on the man leaning over her as she experienced what would fill the rest of her life with nightmares. Her futile struggle stopped only when she lost consciousness.

Gentle readers! It will serve no purpose to describe what happened next. To ask the caste or religion of the men who violated the girl will be as meaningless as asking about her own caste or religion. There is no need either to learn the details of how the girl—once she became conscious again—reached home in her tattered, flour-covered clothes. Certainly there is no need to ask: Were there only cowards in that lane that they— from behind their doors and windows—saw those beasts snatch the girl but only closed their shutters more tightly? What I mean is simply this: Irrespective of her caste or religion, a curfew can deprive any girl of her life's tenderest experience. It can knock her down to the level of animals and drag her through experiences that could turn the rest of her life into an inescapable labyrinth of nightmares.

6

The worst tragedy in the world for a mother is to have her child die in her lap. It occurred a few hours ago in that hellish home consisting of just a room and a veranda. For the adults in that family, it was a familiar experience. Every other year or so, a child died in that family—or in some family nearby. In fact, given all the hunger and ignorance in that lane, it was more surprising that some children actually survived. So, for the older family members, the child's death was almost a natural event, but the children and Sayeeda were shaken to the core.

The corpse, little more than two feet long, lay in the middle of the room, covered with a piece of torn white cloth. The adults were sprawled on the floor around the room, leaning against the walls. Sayeeda's elder daughter, who had just turned three and a half, sat fixedly staring at her dead sister. For the first time in her experience her baby sister was silent—she had always seen her either whining or crying. She even asked her mother, 'Ammi, why doesn't *bahina* speak today?' It made Sayeeda burst into such loud wailing that the girl was horrified and didn't ask again. She felt she had asked something that she shouldn't have. Her seven-year-old cousin was the other member of the family whom the death had disturbed badly. For the two of them, the little girl had been like a toy. After her birth, they had started to think of themselves as grown-ups. Sayeeda, being always busy with household chores, used to let them take care of her little daughter. They hated the baby's whining and crying but still treated her the way the grown-ups did. They would bang a tray or rattle a metal cup to distract her; or, putting her in their lap, they would try to feed her some milk or water with a spoon.

The baby had died just as the day was ending. Gradually it turned dark, and night took hold of that home just as tightly as it had the city all around. Two lights lit the house: one in the room where the family lived and made bidis, the other in the back veranda where it also provided light to the kitchen and the latrine. In the dim light of two cheap bulbs, the people in the house seemed more like phantom figures in some illustration of a magic tale than humans.

Nights of bereavement pass excruciatingly slowly, as if Time itself has come to a stop. Tonight was such a night for the people in that house. The two children, after having vainly struggled to understand the mystery of death, had eventually collapsed to the floor and gone to sleep. They hadn't had anything to eat since noon. Hunger kept them awake long enough, but sleep is children's best friend, and gradually they sank into its lap. Whether in response to the wailing of the women or due to their own hunger pangs, their little eyes had shed enough tears to leave streaks on their grimy cheeks.

Sayeeda's old father-in-law looked remotely in the air; he was silent, lost in thought. Except for the time when his own father had died, he had never been much bothered by any death.

He had been close to his father and was old enough to know what death meant when the latter passed away. His father had also loved him a lot. After toiling all day at making bidis, his father would take him out for a walk—a privilege as the youngest child. When they returned, his hands would be full of colourful marbles or kites, and his mouth would be stuffed with sweet-and-sour lemon drops. He would sit in the middle of the small room, tying a string to the kite or playing with marbles; around him his brothers would continue busily making bidis, frequently casting jealous glances at him. He never felt again what he had felt at his father's death. In subsequent years, death became for him something cold and determined. In his neighbourhood, almost everyone—once they reached the age of twenty-five—would come down with TB. Their damp house, if not the tobacco, would do them in. Though plenty of children were born, they also died in large numbers. Death had become so familiar to him that the little girl's passing away today had, in fact, affected him very little. What had him really worried was the child's burial: How would they get the corpse to the graveyard? He had no hope that the curfew would be lifted during the night, nor could he be sure about the following day. Who could know these things? He had seen what had happened to his son in the morning, how he had rushed inside, cursing and swearing, water splashing out of the buckets in his hands— he must have been assaulted by the police. Meanwhile, the heat and humidity meant that the body had to be buried before the day got too hot; otherwise it was bound to start smelling.

The old man had experienced other curfews. He knew that on such occasions a magistrate would hold office at the Kotwali to issue curfew passes. But it was not easy for someone like him to get a pass. The last few times he had tried he had come back empty-handed. He wanted his son to go, and several times tried to ask him; each time his courage failed him seeing the look on his son's face.

Sayeeda's husband was his father's second child—but the first son. Consequently, he had aged before his time by a sense of responsibility. His awareness of himself as the eldest son affected him so deeply that, by the time he reached his early teens, he was well on his way to turning into a bidi-making machine. He never sneaked out and played carom or chess with other boys, nor did he ever run off to the sandy bank of the river to chase kites. His excessive sense of responsibility had made him look so overbearingly serious that no one could get a sense of exactly how he felt in his heart. No member of the family dared speak to him about anything they thought he might not like. Today he had gone to the veranda at the back—away from their eyes—and shed his tears by himself—it, too, had been a big surprise to his family. They couldn't imagine that he would weep over the loss of a child whom he had scarcely ever fondled in his arms. The tears had washed away the severity of his looks. His face was like an unblemished slate on which they could see every line drawn by his grief. It was perhaps this deceptively settled look that finally gave his father the courage to speak to him.

'We'll have to get a pass.'

'Who'll go to get it?'

'You. Who else?'

'I won't.'

'Why?'

Again the silence that everyone feared. Today, however, it was quickly broken—by Sayeeda. Normally she rarely uttered a word in front of her in-laws; for her to talk to her husband in their presence was even more inconceivable. But her grief forced her to transgress the rules today. She was still in anguish thinking that had some man in the family shown a little courage and got the baby's medicine, her little darling might still be alive. Now this fresh cowardice of her husband threatened even the possibility of a decent burial.

'Hey maula . . . my *bitiya* didn't get any medicine when she lived . . . Won't she now get a decent grave? . . . Hey maula . . . why did you send that poor baby to this home?'

Sayeeda's loud wails broke her father-in-law's will. He was a religious man who prayed and fasted whenever the toils of earning a living allowed him. The mere thought that his grandchild might not even get a proper burial was unbearable to him. He slowly looked at all the members of the family. Every tired, beaten face was turned to the floor. They avoided each other's eyes as they grimly tried to ignore Sayeeda's laments.

'Oh my little golden bird . . . house? . . . She didn't get any milk. Now she won't get even a little grave . . . Won't she now, oh my maula?'

The old man could not bear it any longer. He stared at his wife, expecting some moral support from her at least. Their eyes met a couple of times, but she immediately turned away and looked elsewhere. He checked the time: it was already a little past 7.00 p.m. He didn't know what the current arrangements were, but he remembered last year's curfew. You couldn't easily find any issuing officer after 7.30 p.m. or 8.00 p.m. He had to leave the house immediately. With uncertain legs, and weaker will, he stood up. One of his legs had gone to sleep. He massaged it for a while—even pinched it hard a few times—to bring it back to life. Next he put on his kurta, taking it off the peg on the wall. Finally, after carefully lighting a bidi, he opened the front door with a jerk and stepped out.

The dark-filled outside was like a placid but deep lake; he took his first step into it and kept sinking. No signs of life were visible. Other nights that lane rattled with noises; tonight it was dead silent. The endless line of charpoys was nowhere to be seen. It was the same narrow lane where on other nights you couldn't walk without bumping into something or someone; but now it felt like an open street.

Even normally the public lighting in that lane was insufficient. Tonight, even the light that used to come from the houses could only faintly sneak through the chinks in their closed windows and doors. He kept moving in the darkness, for he knew his way. He had always lived in these lanes. Of course, he changed houses a few times, but it was always in the same neighbourhood. The lanes were spread out like a web for miles. If a stranger ever got lost in them, he could spend hours trying to find his way back to some main street. But it was the old man's familiar world—he could stroll through it even in the dark.

Tonight, however, it was different. A chilling silence filled the lanes. Then there were the police pickets posted wherever several lanes intersected or where a lane opened on to the main street. They would frequently blow their whistles or, if they saw someone at a distance, sound their lathis against the paving and, loudly swearing, chase after him. The old man was deathly scared of them. He chose a long circuitous route that, in the dark, seemed endless, though the Kotwali was barely a kilometre from his house. He had almost reached there when he was caught.

This is what happened. He finally had to leave the lanes and take the main road. From what he could see of the road, it was clear of any human presence. He couldn't hear any noises either. But no sooner had he taken a few steps down the road than a shower of abuses fell upon him. His feeble body made a ludicrous attempt to run, but a lathi struck his legs and he fell down. As he was falling he realized where he had erred. Next to the mouth of the lane, hidden by the columns of a veranda, some policemen had seated themselves on the front ledge of a shuttered shop. They were tired and had been nodding. That's why he had not heard them.

Either it was his age or the terror that had taken hold of his heart, but the old man couldn't get up. He lay there on the ground, sweat and drool dripping from his beard, his scared brimming eyes fixed on the policemen, awaiting the next blow. But it never came. Perhaps his decrepit condition made the jawans less dutiful. Only the man who had thrown his lathi at him kept swearing as he walked over. The others remained seated—tired and bored.

'Mother f . . . ! Walking around in the curfew . . . did your doctor ask you?'

The old man's lips trembled in an effort to say something but only a meaningless whine came out.

'Speak up, saley . . . you don't have a bomb tucked away somewhere, do you? . . . There's no trusting the Musallas. *Diwanji*, should I search him?'

'Go ahead . . . but first ask him where he was going.'

'Where were you going? . . . Speak up!'

The old man again tried to say something, but his voice was too distorted for anyone to understand. The constable grabbed him by the collar and pulled him up. His hands folded and trembling, the old man made another pitiful attempt, but again nothing intelligible came out.

'F . . . your sister! Speak up . . . or should I give you . . . ' The constable raised his arm.

The old man covered his face with his hands, but the constable didn't hit him. He continued to curse and threaten. Finally, the old man managed to say something comprehensible.

'*Sarkar*, I need to get a pass. There's a corpse to be buried. My granddaughter . . . she passed away.'

'What?' The constable stepped back a little.

'You aren't lying, are you?' another constable asked. 'We'll check right now. If it turns out you're lying, I'll stuff this up your arse.' He swung his cane.

'Come, sahib, look for yourself. The house is not far.'

The diwan in charge of the police party was a decent man. When he saw the argument could take a turn for the worse, he quietly said, 'Bhaiya, let him go. This can happen to anyone.'

'*Katuas!* . . . The bastards do nothing but produce children, like mice . . . then they go and die. Hey you, now run off. But if you come back without a pass you know your "daddy" will be waiting for you. *Sala!*'

The old man was in no condition to run, but, considering his age, what his shaking legs did next could hardly be called running. He stumbled, almost fell down, then recovered, then stumbled again, and thus eventually reached the Kotwali.

The scene at the Kotwali was just like last year. The road was packed with the vehicles of the police department, the PAC and the fire brigade. Everywhere outside the shuttered shops—on benches, cold stoves and little ledges—were seated small clusters of jawans. Every so often a stir would pass through them as some senior officer's car would arrive, then they would quickly sink back into their fatigue and boredom.

Inside the Kotwali, in a little room in one corner, a 'lady' magistrate was issuing curfew passes. The room and the veranda outside rocked with noise like a fish market. It was crowded with touts, political leaders, journalists and self-appointed 'social workers' as well as with distressed people of every kind. While the former were grabbing fistfuls of signed passes and passing them on to cronies, the latter had to beg and plead and cajole to get a single pass. The old man too joined the crowd of those who were getting no one's help but everyone's shoves and curses.

He belonged to the country's vast majority for whom honour and insult are meaningless words, and in whom meekness and humility are irrevocably ingrained—who are abused and rejected all their lives and very often lose even their status as human beings. The old man too was tossed around by the milling crowd, abused, shouted at, pushed and shoved; still he somehow managed to get close to the magistrate's desk.

'Name? . . . Quick, speak up . . . I can't keep asking you your name for hours.' The magistrate's irritated voice jogged the old man into full awareness.

'Abdur Rashid . . . Abdur Rashid.'

'Reason?'

'Ji . . . ?'

'What's this *ji ji?* Tell me why you want a pass.'

'The granddaughter passed away. She's to be buried.'

'Oh . . .' The voice softened for the first time.
'How old was she?'

The old man remained silent. He felt no desire to recall his dead granddaughter's age.

'How many persons will go?'

'Seven or eight.'

'Why that many? Two should be enough.' The voice was again irritated and angry.

The old man did what all people of his world do on such occasions. First he lamely tried to argue his case; then, after being severely rebuked, he began to plead and beg and whine. When that too didn't work, he tried to fall at the magistrate's feet. Finally, scolded and cursed, he left the room, his fist tightly closed over a pass for three persons, valid the next morning.

On the way back he was stopped by the police a couple of times, but the pass had filled him with a special kind of confidence—even though it was severely shaken a few times. Once, a policeman grabbed the pass, turned it over and over to examine it, then threatened to tear it up. Another time, a jawan actually threw the pass in the air and let it fall in the dirt. But that new confidence—and his abject humility—still let him reach home, slowly, but certainly.

Home was like a still pond; his arrival started a few little waves on its surface. The adults had stayed awake waiting for him. The moment he cautiously knocked, his wife opened the door as if she had been standing right against it. It made him angry—Why didn't she first ask who it was?—but he let it go.

'Did you get it?' the old woman asked when he stepped inside.

'Yes. For three persons. We'll have to find the *maulvi sahib* in the morning.'

'Just three? What about the *kul*? [certain special prayers said for the benefit of the deceased, usually on the third day or later.]'

Sayeeda, who had been resting her head on her knees, looked up at her mother-in-law's sharp tone. She thought her father-in-law had returned empty-handed and started her wailing again.

'Hey maula . . . won't my bitiya get even a handful of dirt?'

'Shut up, sali,' Sayeeda's husband cut her short with a curse. 'She'll get plenty of dirt. Go and dump on her all the dirt you want in the morning.'

In everything that had happened, he had emerged looking like a coward in front of his wife—it made him feel violent, almost barbaric. For otherwise, he was a quiet person and had never sworn at her before. But was it really a sense of shame at being seen as a coward by his wife that had so enraged him, or was it his frustration at not having been able to do anything for his dying child? He might even have hit Sayeeda had she not immediately understood what was happening to him and shut up.

The brief stir caused by the old man's return soon ended. The voices quieted down and silence returned to the room. Its occupants went back to their places against the walls—except for Sayeeda's mother-in-law who was busily rummaging through the family's meagre boxes. Finally she managed to find a piece of white linen. Actually, it was not quite white now— time had discoloured it—but the old woman knew that she could not hope to find something more suitable for the shroud. She sat down with that piece of cloth and picked up her scissors.

The night had to pass, but for the eyes that could not find sleep it was like a painful debt that had to be paid bit by bit. The little corpse lay in the middle of the room; nearby were sprawled the two sleeping children. If the corpse's face had not been covered, it too would have looked like the two living faces. The adults had had nothing to eat since that morning. And they, of course, had been most frugal with water. Now their guts were crying out for food and their throats were parched. It was a household where one had to earn daily in order to eat daily. During curfews, they would start starving by the second or third day. So the matter of showing respect to death by not having a meal did not arise—they could not have had much of a meal anyway. Sprawled against the walls, they kept thinking about the next day: What if the curfew isn't lifted? For if that were to happen, even the children may have to go without food by the next evening.

In the half light of a solitary bulb the night passed slowly in that room. Outside, in the lane, the tramp of policemen's boots sounded once or twice. A few times some shouts, coming from far away, were also heard. It wasn't clear what the people were shouting: 'Har Har Mahadeo' or 'Allah-o-Akbar'? The occupants of the room lay on the dirty floor, apart from each other, hiding their eyes from each other, being as unobtrusive as possible, while slowly—very slowly—the night passed.

7

At three in the afternoon, with the worst of the heat still continuing, there was an outage.

By then three different crowds had gathered in the Kotwali. One room, where the 'lady' magistrate sat, was packed with people in need of curfew passes. They were piling upon each other and spilling out into the veranda. So much shouting was going on that no one could be understood. When the power went out and the ceiling fan stopped, the room became a mini battlefield.

In the room next to it, when the fan stopped turning, the assembled newsmen stopped discussing the riot and started cursing the electricity department. They had been summoned there by the highest authorities of the district for a briefing scheduled at 3.00 p.m. It was 3.30 p.m. now, but the officers had not arrived. Now the power was gone. The newsmen grumbled noisily. The junior officers, who had hovered around trying to keep the former entertained, slipped away one by one. The journalists talked about boycotting the press conference but remained seated. Today their own interest was at stake. They had no intention of walking away no matter how long the delay. Any other time, most of them would have stomped off, leaving the junior officers begging in their trail.

The third crowd, gathered in the inner yard of the Kotwali, consisted of the people who had been invited to attend the 'Peace Committee' meeting: politicians, doctors, lawyers, social workers and other such professionals. They were invited to these meetings whenever there was a riot—or a major festival. Their expressions were so predictable and their words so trite that the Kotwali walls—if they could speak—could have poured forth those worthies' speeches verbatim.

Like in other years, this year too, when the rioting started, the district authorities first issued an order that not even a bird should be seen on any road—anyone who broke the law would be skinned alive. Then ministers began to arrive from the capital to tour the city and complaints were made to them that 'the administration was not utilizing the cooperation offered by the people's representatives'. Late the first night, therefore, the district officers decided to call a meeting of the Peace Committee and constables rushed around from dawn till noon, to inform its members. So it was that for a meeting scheduled for 3.00 p.m., some ten or fifteen people had assembled by 3.30 p.m. Stragglers still kept coming. Each said the same thing on arrival: he received the news very late, but right away he had slipped on his kurta—or chappals—and rushed over. These meetings never started on time. Everyone expected that people would keep coming in for another hour or so. That was what the officers had in mind to begin with: they wished to start the peace meeting after their own press conference.

When the power went off, the last two groups began to scatter and mingle. The stifling heat made it impossible for people to remain seated inside. The journalists came out and stood around in several small groups in the veranda. The chief topics were again the origins of the riot and the failure of the authorities to stop it.

Munshi Harprasad was an old freedom fighter and for the past twenty years had been the local correspondent of an English daily published from the capital. Though seventy, he was still fully active. People liked to say things to get a rise out of him. In response, Munshiji would sometimes make such a brutally frank remark that his detractor would be left silently fuming while others would have a hard time suppressing laughter. Today he seemed unusually silent. A newsman tried the old gambit.

'What's the matter, Munshiji? You look rather run down today.'

'Run down? Not in the least.' Munshiji first tried to end the matter there, then changed his mind—he knew his reticence would only bring him more questions. 'I was thinking,' he continued, 'if this *Shankarji's* marriage party that has been summoned here in the name of the Peace Committee were all locked up under MISA [Maintenance of Internal Security Act], the rioting might immediately stop.'

There was a loud guffaw. Many members of the Peace Committee had joined the newsmen on the veranda; some of them pretended not to have heard Munshiji's remark, others writhed silently, but those with thicker skins joined the general laughter.

'Why only us, Munshiji? You should lock up some of your journalist brethren, too. Don't they smack their lips when they publish the gory news? Where there's one death, they see twenty corpses. If a firecracker goes off, they announce it was a bomb. Put them in jail with us—then the riot will stop.'

That caused a bit of an uproar. From the freedom of the press to the sharing of power with the masses, all sorts of issues were loudly debated. But not for long. Soon the two groups were cracking jokes again as mere individuals. Most of them knew each other well and were long accustomed to ribbing each other.

Munshiji began to feel depressed again. Earlier that day he had toured the riot-affected area, and the sights of violence and pillage had left him deeply disturbed. The almost obscene bantering going on between the Peace Committee people and the newsmen further worsened his mood. A small group of four journalists from Delhi was recognizable by the clothes and cameras. The visitors considered themselves different from the local scribes and were standing at a distance from them. Earlier, they too had made the rounds of the neighbourhoods with Munshiji. Now the latter, without much enthusiasm, walked over and joined them.

'Munshiji, it's *horrible*. The city has suffered a major *tragedy*, yet look at the *sensibility* of these journalists. How *shamelessly* they laugh!'

Munshi Harprasad's eyes narrowed as he listened to the jeans-clad girl. He was afraid he might throw up. These boys and girls had toured the affected areas with him. At the sight of any burned-down house or a bone sticking out from a smouldering pile, they had expressed their grief and pain in English. Then, when the sun had turned hot, they had an icebox taken out from the back of the Information Officer's jeep and into the veranda of a half-burned house, where they had refreshed themselves with chilled beer—while Munshiji had stayed with the driver and angrily kept pressing the horn. Now this girl was calling his colleagues 'shameless' and 'insensitive'!

Only Comrade Surajbhan caught on to what was happening to Munshiji. They had been friends for decades. He knew well that Munshi Harprasad was not just another 'pen-pusher', that he was affected by news and often, working on some story, could himself become a part of it. He walked over to Munshiji and, grabbing his hand, gently led him away.

Suddenly a loud voice was heard at the other end of the veranda, and everyone's attention turned that way. Lala Radhey Lal, owner of Khemchand Jugalkishore & Co., had been teased once too often and struck back like an irate cobra.

'Yes, it's true. The grain prices will rise and I'll make some profit. But who hates a profit? I'm, however, not so low that I'd start a riot just to increase my receipts. But you, Sharmaji, you can do even that. Don't you know the difference between a Pakistani flag and the flag of the Muslim League? And you know equally well that the local office of the Muslim League is in Khuldabad, right next to that mosque. Even then you published a picture of the League flag and captioned it: "Pakistani flag flies over a mosque." Now you tell me who's starting a riot, you or I?'

'But, guru, once a riot starts, it's only you who rake in money.'

'Sure, and why not? People are assholes. They riot; we make a few paisas.'

There was a loud burst of laughter. A few more vulgar jokes were exchanged and the tension began to subside.

Meanwhile, there was that first crowd of pass-seekers. They didn't leave the room even after the outage, but went on arguing and pleading with the 'lady' magistrate and her two assistants. The magistrate was fresh in the service and still quite young; as such, unlike her more senior colleagues, she still had some feelings of empathy and idealism left in her. She wanted to do something. She didn't think that common people were ignorant fools. So she toiled away, dripping with perspiration. Every once in a while she would snap at someone, but her fingers never stopped. Her assistants complained about the heat and the crush of people; but seeing her lack of concern, they dared not step out.

Some of those who had come for the Peace Committee meeting were members of the local municipal board. Since their elections were not too far away, they were quick to perceive future votes in the pass-seekers. Immediately, each of them grabbed his own constituents and barged into the crowd. That completely upset everything. The magistrate's voice became louder and angrier. She raised her head to look at the 'leaders' who were shoving and shouting, and suddenly realized how much stuffier the room had become. Slapping the files shut, she announced that the work would be resumed only when the power came back. It was the chance her subordinates needed; they immediately fled the room.

The fact that the magistrate was a woman stumped the 'leaders' for a few seconds; then they resumed their shouting:

'It's this bureaucracy, sahib, that has ruined the country. First they start a riot, then they treat the *janata* like animals.'

'*Aji*, when there is a riot their income goes up. You know the saying, "Give out relief funds, rake in money." Don't we know who skims off the cream from the milk that is being distributed since yesterday?'

'*Arrey*, even now, you only need to hand out a hundred and you'll get your pass all right—outage or no outage.'

'What? What did you say? I'm asking for money!' sputtered the magistrate, her face turning red with anger. She wanted to say more but her voice choked. Her chaprasi brought a couple of police constables and together they escorted her into another room.

Being new to the job, the magistrate didn't know how to deal with such a situation. The 'leaders' were all old hands; they knew how to gang up on an officer and make fun of him. Between the two—the magistrate and the 'leaders'—were the bedraggled, bewildered people who didn't know when they could hope to get a curfew pass. Some had a sick child at home. Others needed to catch a train. Still others had other needs. But they could only wait—that was the only choice they had.

'*Excuse me*, Munshiji. What's this concerning some flag?' The young men and women from Delhi surrounded Munshiji.

'Flag . . . what flag?' Munshiji pretended ignorance.

'Someone was just saying that the local press published a picture of the Muslim League flag but called it the flag of Pakistan.'

Munshiji remained silent; he didn't want to get involved in a local dispute. It was Comrade Surajbhan who answered the question, 'Bhai—sorry, I don't know your name, but whoever you are—let me tell you, your capital papers haven't been any less mischievous. You always find some Pakistani hand behind every riot. There hasn't been a riot since Independence in which more Muslims have not been killed, but each time you publish the news as if there's been a massacre of Hindus. When Muslims complain of the high-handedness of the police or the PAC, you call them traitors. The press people here are merely your younger brothers. The local office of the Muslim League is right next to that mosque. It had the party flag flying on the roof. A little trick photography moved the flag to the mosque itself. Your friends lost nothing when they called it a Pakistani flag. It didn't hurt them one bit that their words increased the tension in the city. Delhi or Lucknow, most of the people in this business wear khaki shorts under their white trousers.' [Follow the RSS or the extreme Hindu nationalist line.]

Now it was Munshi Harprasad's turn. He pressed Comrade Surajbhan's arm to divert his attention and pulled him away from the people from Delhi. The latter looked rather dismayed. They were itching to make a retort and felt cheated now that Comrade had been dragged away.

The power and the senior officers returned simultaneously, and the press conference started.

'What's the total number of casualties?'

'Six.'

'How many bodies were thrown into the canal?'

'...'

'How do you count the casualties?'

'The dead bodies are brought to the mortuary for a post-mortem . . .'

'What about those that didn't get there? That were thrown in the canal. How . . . ?'

Just then trays of cold drinks, samosas and *barfi* were brought in. In between munching and sipping, complaints were aired. 'Why was there a delay in issuing passes to the journalists?' 'Why were they provided only the one "push-and-ride" jeep of the Information Department?' 'How was it that even that battered vehicle was then commandeered by the Delhiwallas, while the local people had to trudge around on foot?' The officers sent for some more samosas.

'These riots *wiots* . . . they'll go on happening. What about the Journalists' Colony? It's been delayed already by the riot. You really must allot the plots as soon as things calm down.'

'Yes, yes . . . we'll take care of it. We'd have done it by now if this trouble hadn't started. The land's been set aside. It's right in the middle of the Civil Lines area. All that's needed is to divide it into plots. That we can do the moment this trouble ends.'

Some of the journalists had not yet put in their applications. They loudly claimed that they had not been informed of the deadline. They were told that they could put in backdated applications. Several immediately tore out pages from their notebooks and got going.

The officers then divided up the journalists into several small groups and explained to them how the events were to be reported.

Munshi Harprasad and Comrade Surajbhan left the room and walked out into the courtyard. The latter had joined the press conference just for the heck of it; actually, he was there for the Peace Committee meeting. Now he went over to that area and took his friend along with him. Most of the committee members were hanging around in the courtyard and verandas. Some had gone over to get curfew passes; still others lurked outside the room where the press conference was going on. What else could they do? They had to wait for the same senior officers to come and conduct the Peace Committee meeting.

The two friends pulled aside a couple of chairs and sat down. Again some people gathered around them and the talk returned to the same topics: how the riot started, how many people had died, how much property had been destroyed.

'No matter who started the trouble,' Comrade Surajbhan said in sorrowful tones, 'one thing has now become clear. When there were similar riots at the time of Independence, lots of people would stand up to the troublemakers. Now their number seems to decline every year.'

'Aji, now even your neighbour doesn't protect you. Earlier you could be sure that at least he wouldn't attack you. Now even that isn't certain.'

'Take Rampal Singh; he's an old communist. A "cardholder" for some twenty years. His son was killed in one of the riots. I went to offer my condolences—I tell you I was struck dumb. Such a fine man has turned communal. He was openly saying nasty things about Muslims. I said to him, "Comrade, you shouldn't condemn the Muslims. You should rather condemn the *tendencies* that cause riots." But did he listen to me? It seems the whole city has been cut up into Hindus and Muslims.'

Munshi Harprasad placed a hand on Comrade Surajbhan's shoulder. He could understand his pain. Many a long evening he had seen him argue fiercely with his colleagues. Often, late at night, his friend had come to his house and cried, 'It's all coming to an end, Munshiji. The comrades who fought communalism for decades have suddenly themselves become fanatics.'

Munshiji would listen silently, shaking his head in disbelief. He himself had seen how even those who in previous riots had enthusiastically taken out 'peace marches' and gone around their neighbourhoods educating people, had now become Hindus and Muslims. But it was something recent, this increasing mistrust of one's own neighbour. For the first time ever, he had seen people attack their own neighbours and plunder their homes. Perhaps it was the ultimate end of the bitter divide that he had seen gradually developing over the years between the two communities.

As soon as the district officers entered the marquee where the Peace Committee was to meet, the committee members wandering around also started drifting back. Some of the journalists joined them too.

'Respected DM sahib, honourable SP sahib, other high officers of the district, enlightened citizens of our city, brothers and sisters! Every meeting needs a president, and so I submit to you the name of Mukherji Dada to preside over this meeting.'

'I second it.'

Before the sentence could end, Mukherji Dada was up and in the presidential chair. He had been presiding over these meetings for more than a decade and always came prepared. Others had grown so accustomed to it that they regarded his presidentship as an inevitable part of the proceedings.

Mukherji Dada sat in the middle, with the DM on one side and the SP on the other. Two MLAs and an MP, and a few other 'dignitaries' also joined them on the stage. The proceedings started. The gentleman who had offered Mukherji Dada's name in nomination was Majid Sahib, a lawyer by profession and the permanent 'conductor' of these meetings. He now picked up the mike and began with a speech of his own. People were sick and tired of this habit of his. Before inviting a speaker to the mike, he would always make long, introductory remarks, interspersed with bits of poetry. Then, as the speaker would hurry to the mike, he would repeatedly warn him to watch his time. Most speakers never paid any attention to his instructions and sometimes scuffles broke out over who should have the microphone.

Today too, Majid Sahib quoted several Urdu verses and reminded his audience that their 'flower garden' needed 'red roses', not 'red blood'. Only when his audience began to make loud remarks did he start inviting speakers to the mike.

There was a *kanat* stretched behind the stage, behind which the more junior civil and police officers were relaxing in chairs. They could hear the speeches, but their own whispered comments could not reach their superiors' ears. Whenever a speaker would solemnly appeal at the top of his voice that the city had to be saved from being burned down, they would mutter nastily.

'Sala! Now he's preaching peace. Back in his lane he'll hand out knives to his goons.'

'If only we could put these bastards behind bars—the riot would stop in no time.'

'But how can we? The bosses invite them to the Kotwali and serve them tea and samosas—as if to their sons-in-law.'

'Do they have a choice? If they don't, the minister's stick will be up their own asses.'

Their remarks and laughter sometimes got loud and reached the ears of the people on the stage. Then one of the latter would glare at them briefly, and they would fall silent, conspiratorially pressing each other's hands. But a few moments later their whispers and giggles would start again.

'*Bhaiyo*, as I said before, the bureaucracy of our country thinks of us only when the situation gets totally out of control. I said it before: When the garden needed it, we offered it our blood. But now that spring is here, they ask us: Who are you? They didn't invite us earlier. But now that they have, we'll tell them how to control the riot . . .'

'Sure, *beta*, tell them. Who else if you won't?'

The whisper from the back was loud enough to be heard by everyone—except the speaker at the mike. The officers on the stage smiled. Some of the men in the front row below grinned. But the speaker was not fazed.

'Yes, as I was saying, my brothers who say things against the police and the PAC are only destroying the strength of our country. They're the agents of the CIA and the PLO . . .'

'PLO? When did they start inciting riots in India?'

'Not the PLO. I mean . . . China . . . no, I mean Japan . . .'

'Who cares what you mean!'

There was a brief rumpus, then the proceedings continued and another speaker was called to the mike. Such things commonly happened at these meetings. No one paid them much attention. Except for the speaker himself, no one ever had any interest in what was being said. When a joke was told or a verse quoted, perhaps then some of them paid some attention; otherwise the speakers and the listeners remained separately engrossed in themselves.

Pandit Ayodhyanath Dixit represented the city in the Legislative Assembly. He had been on the stage but, after his own speech, had come down. At the moment he was very worried. The riot was a threat to his political survival. There had been a riot around the time of the previous elections too, but that had gone in his favour. This time, his old rival, Ram Krishna Jaiswal, was reaping the benefit. And the elections were terribly close. Dixitji was sure that the riot had been instigated by Ram Krishna Jaiswal. Jaiswal was a staunch *hinduvadi*. But he also had close ties with Haji Badruddin, the bidi tycoon. Everyone knew that together the two could start a riot any time they wished. The main danger from a riot too close to the elections was that it would divide the voters into Hindus and Muslims. The Muslims would all seek shelter behind Haji Badruddin, while the Hindus, looking for a Hindu leader, would come together behind Jaiswal. And who would be hurt but Pandit Ayodhyanath Dixit.

Dixitji joined some of his supporters standing in a corner of the marquee. He was not conversing with them as much as he was venting his rage against Ram Krishna Jaiswal and his presence on the stage.

'Sala! See how he's all smiles talking to the collector. And this damned collector . . . I must deal with him. Did you see how he invited Jaiswal to come and sit on the stage? *Badmash!* He must go before the elections are announced. Doesn't he know the riot was organized by Jaiswal and Haji Badruddin? I had told him, "Don't invite the two to the Peace Committee meeting." But he not only invited them but also asked them to sit with him on the stage!'

That was why, in his speech that day, Dixitji had criticized the district administration a great deal. 'No "relief" has been distributed.' 'The city is overflowing with garbage.' 'The people are crying for basic needs.' Surrounded by his supporters and forgetting that he was still at a public meeting, Dixitji continued with his diatribe.

Ram Krishna Jaiswal and Haji Badruddin were enjoying Dixitji's discomfort. Every so often they knowingly winked at each other. They also put on deliberate smiles and repeatedly leaned over to whisper something or the other to the collector. Dixitji watched them from a distance and ground his teeth. 'Yes, the moment the riot ends, I'll have him transferred.'

The collector knew what was going on. He kept glancing at Dixitji as he tried to avoid the confidences of Jaiswal and Badruddin. But the two kept leaning over every few minutes to whisper something innocuous in his ears, and he had no choice but to nod in assent. He was desperately seeking some excuse to move away from the two. At some point, the SP had moved to the end of the row. The collector gestured to him to exchange seats with him, but the SP pretended not to understand. He was enjoying the discomfort of his colleague, who had recently caused him some grief by complaining to various ministers that he was not getting full cooperation from the police. The collector had also used certain journalists whom he favoured to plant unfavourable news. Consequently, the SP had also started privately briefing his own trustworthy group of newsmen. Pandit Ayodhyanath Dixit belonged to the party currently in power. The SP realized that he could use him to get at the collector. He quietly beckoned to one of his subordinates, then whispered to him to ask Dixit to see him after the meeting. The subordinate delivered the message. All this did not escape the collector. He saw everything and began to plan his own new strategy to deal with the SP.

The speeches had gone on for so long that, except for those who had yet to speak, everyone else had no endurance left. Even the hosts were bored stiff. Some of the people on the stage started whispering to Majid Sahib, who kept nodding in agreement. But each time a speech ended, he merely stepped to the mike, recited a few couplets and invited the next speaker on his list. The collector finally spoke to him with some force. Majid Sahib promptly invited Mukherji Dada to come to the mike and present his presidential remarks. Immediately, the dignitaries who were thus denied their chance to speak began to shout in protest. Some of them even rushed to the mike and said what they wanted to say. No one, of course, understood them—there was so much noise and confusion. It was only with great difficulty that the president finally got hold of the mike.

Mukherji Dada's presidential remarks were well known; his audience had heard them several times during the past several years. Everyone knew when they could expect to hear a joke, when they must applaud in support, and when they should cry, 'Shame ! Shame!' in condemnation. On the few occasions when Mukherji Dada's memory failed him, the audience easily reminded him of his own words. That is why, before his speech actually came to an end, the people were already standing up. Mukherji Dada's final sentences were completely lost in the noise of tumbling chairs and hurrying feet. Tea had been laid out in a smaller tent nearby, and that was where everyone dashed to.

Between gulps of tea and bites of samosas, nasty gossip and abject sycophancy continued. Leaders, administrators, newsmen, social workers—everyone vented their jealous animosity and denigrated others. No one missed the smallest chance to conspire and push for his own gain. There was bound to be a riot every couple of years—why worry too much about it?

8

House searches had been going on and had by now become routine. When the army was on duty, they used to do it, otherwise the civil authorities always asked the BSF or the CRP to surround the 'Pakistani' neighbourhood of the city. Then the police and the PAC jawans did the searches. The authorities firmly believed that it was the people of that neighbourhood who unfailingly started every riot. That's why they always searched only that area—even when all the casualties would be from there. It happened this year too when all the six people killed were from that neighbourhood. The authorities decided to conduct searches in the 'Pakistani' neighbourhood and put their plan into effect an hour or so after midnight.

The sweat-drenched city, tortured all day by high humid heat, had just been lulled into drowsiness by the slightly cooler night air. Only the people who truly had to earn their bread daily—whose bellies were now on fire from hunger—were still semi-awake; the rest by now were well in the grip of sleep. Earlier, shouts of 'Har Har Mahadeo' and 'Allah-o-Akbar' had swept over the walls and roofs of the neighbourhood in waves, but they too had gradually ended after midnight. These cries always raised a curious mix of excitement and fear in the people who heard them. As they nervously hid in their homes, they felt as if the attackers were shouting next door.

It was past 1.30 a.m. when the sounds of a number of big vehicles stopping on the main roads were heard. Their headlights lit up the dark corners of the roads and lanes. Some of that light fell upon the windows and transoms of the houses, and wafted down inside. Frightened hands immediately closed any open shutter. Then began the rhythmic noise of heavy boots. The jawans ran down the lanes and took up strategic positions, their boots sounding ominously loud in the still night. The scared, not-quite-awake people in the homes began to prepare themselves for the coming onslaught.

'Khat . . . khat . . . thak . . . thak! Open up! Open up, you bastard. Get off your mother's lap. You want me to kick down your door?'

Noises resounded everywhere and filled the air. Noises of fists beating on doors, of boots kicking down doors, of sticks striking human backs and bellies. Triumphant shouts and curses. Cries and screams. Pleading voices. Begging voices. Voices of children and women. This maelstrom of noises appeared suddenly and churned up the entire neighbourhood.

'*Bahanchod!* What took you so long? Hiding away the weapons, were you? Or has someone got your tongue?'

'Speak up, sasur . . . or has someone got your tongue?'

The children were sprawled on the floor overwhelmed by sleep, while the adults huddled against the walls, numb with fear. When the door had burst open, several policemen had rushed in. The men inside instinctively covered their heads with their hands, expecting any moment to be clubbed by rifle butts or kicked by boots. Their expectations would really have been met, had not the scream of a woman torn to shreds the heavy frozen air of the room.

'Hey maula! Would you now have my baby's corpse crushed under these boots?'

The sight of a boot raised dangerously close to the little cloth-covered body had made Sayeeda scream.

'What's that? Whose corpse?'

Sayeeda didn't answer. She had started to wail, and so had her mother- and sister-in-law. It was the old man who somehow explained the situation. The boots rushed out in a hurry. Since the door could not be closed properly, the old man propped its two panels together with the help of a broken table. Now, what was happening outside could no longer be seen—but the outside noises continued to stream in.

'What's in that box? Open it . . . That one too.'

'Hujur . . . mai-bap . . . it's just the girl's trinket and things . . . she'll be married this coming winter . . . '

'Open it! How do I know you don't have a bomb in it? One shouldn't trust you folks anyway. You're always bringing guns and bombs from Pakistan.'

'Open it, saley. We'll be here long after dawn if we have to spend so much time at every house.'

'Now open it nicely, or I'll smash the lock—and your teeth.'

A rifle's butt can smash both. The only difference is that a lock makes a loud noise, but the human mouth makes only a muffled cry.

'Hujur . . . mai-bap . . . we had a hard time getting them . . . now our daughter won't get married . . . '

The infirm, imploring hand placed on the khaki-clad leg dropped to the floor. A second blow of the rifle's butt left it in no condition to grasp at any leg again. Then the boots walked away. The men and women of the house wailed and cried; the children screamed. But all to no avail.

The searches ended exactly the same way at every house. If the dark, dusty faces were not left streaked with tears, they were left twisted with anguish and humiliation, blankly staring after the boots.

'*Abey*, what took you so long to open the door?'

'I was asleep. I came as soon as I could.'

'What! You dare to answer back!' Slap . . . slap.

'Why did you hit me? What gave you the . . . ?'

'Sala, *you* ask about "right"? This gave me the right.'

The rifle's butt partly hit the mouth and partly the door beside it. The mouth spit out some blood—and a few teeth. Some women and older men rushed forward and clung to the young man. The sight of the blood made the patriarch of the house shake with rage. He tried to talk calmly to the magistrate facing him but his voice gradually turned bitter.

'You watch silently while this goes on. Is this how a search is conducted? What law gives you the right to strike people without due cause? I was once a lawyer. This country has a constitution. There are laws . . . there are rules . . . '

'Lawyer's arse! You think you can teach us the law?'

No old mouth ever received a rifle butt and remained to face anything.

'Saley . . . they eat our food but spy for Pakistan. Better search this house carefully. The scoundrel must have a transmitter. Saley! They spread the news . . . that's how the BBC starts blaring it in the morning.'

'Spy for Pakistan . . .' Twisting his crooked and bloodied mouth, the young face muttered, 'I never did it before . . . but now I will. If this is what I get in this f . . . ing country . . .'

'What! What did you say? . . . Spy for Pakistan! Now you'll have to tell us where you've hidden your transmitter.'

The crooked mouth was made a bit more crooked before the women could throw themselves on top of him.

Every time the young man caught sight of his father's torn cheek he writhed with rage. To stop him from saying anything further, the old lawyer and the rest of the family huddled over him on the floor. Some begged him to be quiet; others scolded him. And if ever his voice grew too loud, some woman or another screamed more loudly to keep his words from being heard.

The searchers, however, had lost interest in him. Leaving two jawans to stand guard on the family, the rest had spread over the house. It seemed to be a fairly well-to-do family, consequently everyone was keen to do the searching. Even the two men left behind soon slipped away and joined their colleagues. The members of the household sat down on the sofa and chairs in the front room, and continued to console or hush each other. When the search team finally left, the women rushed inside and, pawing through their plundered boxes, began to cry and scream. Their men scolded them. The old lawyer staggered forward and slammed the outside door shut.

Such scenes were played out in every house, except one. It was a different story at Haji Badruddin's place. His house was spread over two acres of land, surrounded by a high wall. No one standing outside could see what was going on inside. When the police party, led by a deputy collector and a DSP, opened the front gate and entered the lovely grounds, they felt they had stepped from a burning desert into a cool paradise. In the soothing blue light of a tinted bulb, some people were sitting on the lawn beside a line of tall, handsome palm trees.

'What's this crowd doing here during the curfew?' The speaker tried to make his words sound threatening but they had no effect on his listeners—because he burst into laughter even before he finished.

'*Aiye,* huzur . . . please come. What curfew, *dipti* sahib? We're sitting inside our home.'

For a while there was a friendly argument over whether the curfew rules meant 'inside the house itself' or did they mean 'inside the boundary wall'. The jawans dropped down on the steps leading to the terraced lawn and stretched their legs. The officers stepped through the rose beds and sprawled on lawn chairs. Everyone was bone tired and had not had much sleep for a couple of days. The moment they sat down they began to doze off. Haji Badruddin's servants quickly started serving them cold water and lemonade.

'What can I offer you, sahib? This is such a bad time.'

'This is enough, Hajiji. Even this cold water tastes heavenly right now.'

'I have a little bit of the "good stuff" too, sahib. If you'll allow . . . '

'No, no. This is no time for either "good" or "bad".' The deputy collector cast a hurried glance at the subordinates sitting at some distance.

'I'll have things set up inside, sahib. Please do take a little. You'll be refreshed.'

'That's all right, Hajiji. Perhaps some other time.'

Suddenly one of the sub-inspectors noticed that there was someone sprawled in a chair in a shadowy corner of the lawn. The chair was close to the *mehndi* bushes and it was impossible to notice it at first glance. Suddenly alert, he called out, 'Who's there? Who's there near the bushes?'

'Arrey, Jaiswalji, come over here. Come and sit here, otherwise the sahibs might think I have kidnapped a Hindu.'

Ramkrishna Jaiswal—a sheepish look on his face—stepped out of the shadows. He was a former MLA and was planning to contest again in the coming elections. Haji Badruddin was his old rival. But it was currently rumoured in the city that the two had joined hands against the incumbent, Pandit Ayodhyanath Dixit.

'Jaiswalji, what are you doing here so late!' The officer feigned surprise. 'Is everything all right?'

'You know, dipti sahib, I'm worried about the city. So I just slipped through the lanes and came here—to discuss the situation with Hajiji. We were just discussing how to stop the riot when all of you arrived.'

'Sala! How innocently he talks now!' One of the sub-inspectors, seated at a distance, muttered to another next to him. 'Everyone knows the rioting continues because of these two. But who can touch them?'

'Be quiet, *yaar*. Why earn a bad name for nothing? These crooks work behind the scenes. Their money can do anything. Who's going to catch them—and why?' The other sub-inspector responded, struggling to keep his voice down.

The DSP looked into the eyes of the deputy collector. The two stood up and moved away.

'I think, bhai sahib, there's something wrong. Jaiswal's presence here is most suspicious. If you say so, perhaps we should do a search. There may well be something here.'

'Sharmaji, you're talking like a child. You think Haji would keep the weapons in his own house? Or Jaiswal would go around stabbing people himself? It's their money and brains that do the dirty work. Don't expect to find anything here. But if you search this house now, you may as well expect to find us transferred elsewhere tomorrow.'

The two officers continued to talk quietly. It made Haji and Jaiswal, recumbent in their chairs, slightly worried. Jaiswal's nervousness began to show, but Haji kept reassuring him silently.

The two officers walked back and sat down. The chit-chat started again. Jaiswal told them how Hajiji had opened a *langar* to distribute free food to the poor Hindus in his neighbourhood. But his men were having problems getting curfew passes and were unable to bring succour to everyone. Haji, on his part, told them how his friend Jaiswal had given shelter to his Muslim neighbours in his own house. Just then the tea arrived.

'We just had something cold, Hajiji. Why did you trouble yourself further?'

'What trouble, sahib? I, in fact, feel ashamed. You have graced my house at a time when I cannot properly serve you anything.'

'Well, we'll plan something for when we're all more free,' Jaiswal added. *'Begum Sahiba* makes a fine chicken dish. Hajiji, when the curfew ends, you must invite the sahibs for dinner.'

'I'm always ready, Jaiswalji. Whenever.'

'We'll see . . . we'll plan something, Hajiji. But first you should rid us of this curfew soon.'

'Sahib, if you ask us, you may end it today rather than tomorrow. We're ready. We'll make any sacrifice to bring peace to the city.'

'That's true . . . What I meant was that we can have our party only when the riot-mongers give us all a chance.'

The officers stood up. Their subordinates dusted themselves off and grabbed their rifles and canes. The small line of some eight or ten men slowly walked out. Haji Badruddin followed them to the gate where he stopped, raised his hand to his bowed forehead and said, 'If I take another step, I'll have to ask you for a pass.'

Jaiswalji and the officers chuckled. One by one, the jeeps started moving. Hajiji slowly pushed the big gates shut. For some moments, the stillness of the night echoed with the noise of the jeep engines, while the beams of headlights danced oddly on the desolate walls all around.

9

While the tumult outside lasted—the crash and bang of the doors, the crunch and clatter of the boots, the screams of the people—the members of that household remained frozen in fear. The noises meant that the searches were still going on, and these people had already experienced their terrifying efficiency. The searches continued as if there would be no end to them, then gradually things calmed down. After a brief interval, there was the sound of several engines being started simultaneously. It engulfed the lane like the roar of an angry swarm of bees. Then the headlights were turned on and their brilliance bathed the homes. It was only when the lane was sunk in darkness again that its people fully believed that the searches had ended, and began to doze off again.

The rooster in the vegetable-seller's house next door crowed unusually loudly. Perhaps the turmoil of the night had roused its anger. The shrill noise woke Sayeeda's mother-in-law first. The old woman was a light sleeper and last night she had barely had a few winks of sleep. She peered at the clock sitting on the stool in the corner. But the clock was small, and also partly hidden by the *surahi* of water on the stool. The old woman cast a glance around the room. One or two of the people sprawled against the walls were clearly awake, though their eyes were closed, but none of them could be expected to come to her aid.

She got up and, moving aside the *surahi*, checked the time. It was almost 4 a.m. A sudden anxiety gripped her. She shook the surahi. It was empty. There had been no chance to fill it the previous day, and whatever little water had remained in it had been drained out by the children last night. The old woman went into the kitchen. The bucket there still had a couple of mugs left. But the water tap in the house had started making hissing sounds. It meant soon there would be some water. She quickly placed the bucket under the tap and turned the knob all the way open. The latter was, effectively, only a turn of phrase. No matter how wide one opened the faucet, the water always came down in a trickle. You would sooner lose your patience than find your bucket filled to the brim.

The old woman used the water already in the bucket to take care of her morning needs. By the time she stepped out of the latrine, a trickle had started. The old woman sat down near the tap and began the vigil, but the loss of sleep at night soon had her nodding. She woke up again only when her head swayed against the wall. She hurriedly looked up: the bucket was a quarter full. It meant she had had a nice nap. She quickly filled a lota. Lying nearby was a little sliver of soap used for washing clothes. She picked it up and began to rub it on her hands. The sliver was so small that it produced no foam and when the old woman used a little force, it slipped out of her fingers and fell into the drain. Any other day she would have carefully fished it out of the black slush, but it had been a hard night and there was still the little corpse lying inside. She ignored the loss of that tiny piece of soap which she otherwise would have used for another day or two, and which would have drawn from her a torrent of screams had it been dropped by some other member of the family.

The cold water splashed on the arms and face had revived her a little. Rubbing the hands dry on her kurta, she hurried back in. The water could stop soon. If the others took care of themselves quickly, there could be some water to wash the corpse. She knew from her past experience that they couldn't possibly get that much water from their own tap, but the mere thought of going out to the public tap scared her. With all her heart, she wished: let everyone finish fast; may no one need to go outside. They would need water to drink during the day, but that could be taken care of later. The men could get it on their way back from the cemetery.

The others were still asleep, except for the old man. His eyes were open, fixedly staring at something. In fact, looking at the unmoving pupils it was hard to say whether he was awake or merely asleep with open eyes. Sayeeda was leaning against the wall, her head bent to one side. Drool had trickled out of her open mouth and down her chin and left wet spots on her clothes. Her drooling mouth seemed so revolting. The old woman felt a desire to gently wipe away the drool and let Sayeeda sleep a while longer, but she was bound to her habit. So she said, 'Get up, karamjali! You plan to sleep till noon?'

The old woman's voice did not have its usual harsh edge, but it was loud as always. Sayeeda opened her eyes with a start. For a moment she couldn't understand why she was leaning against the wall and tried to get up in a hurry. Then her eyes fell upon the sheet covering the dead child. She began to cry again, first in sobs then openly and loudly. But she had not eaten for the last twenty-four hours and her voice quickly turned hoarse. Soon only sobs issued from her mouth.

Sayeeda's wailing awakened the other adults sprawled on the floor. The children slept on, but the adults sat up. The old woman brusquely told them to get on and be done with the latrine, and they started going to the back veranda one by one.

The tap had remained open, but the bucket filled only once. And now, when even the trickle stopped, there was just a little water left at the bottom—what the old woman had been afraid of. There were still the children: they would need water the moment they got up. And above everything, there was the corpse to be washed. The little girl had been dead for twelve hours. The night had been bad enough, but the day was bound to get much hotter soon and the corpse would begin to smell. The old woman wanted to get it washed right away; then they could start worrying about the burial.

The only water they could now get was outside—the public tap in the lane. Sayeeda's husband had not yet forgotten his experience of the previous morning. As for the old man, his spirit was so shattered last night while getting the pass that he had no courage to go out for water. He could show the pass, but there was no trusting the police. They could tear up his pass and hit him to boot. A wish was restless in one corner of his heart: let the old woman go out to get the water. He did not want any of his sons to go out. In any case, some woman had always fetched water in the morning. It wouldn't be safe today to send out a young woman, but there would be no danger if the old woman went out. In the event, she did.

Holding an empty bucket in each hand, she stepped out, but it took her ages to cover the fifty metres of the desolate lane. Finally she reached close to the corner around which was the public tap. Any other day there would have been a line of empty pots right up to where she stood, but there was no sign of anyone today. The still invisible tap seemed to be going full blast, for she could clearly hear the water. It was only when she turned the corner that she saw the policeman. He was standing at the tap, repeatedly cupping his hands under the gushing water, then splashing and scrubbing his face. The old woman stopped, but only momentarily. Going back was no longer possible; she had to continue. When she reached close to the policeman, she stopped again, scared. His back was towards her. When he turned around, his voice was loud and irritated.

'What are you doing here, *budhiya*? Take the water and run home.'

The old woman did not expect to be let off so easily. She quickly filled the two buckets and rushed home. When she entered the house—a full bucket in each hand—she loftily looked at all the men. Quickly pouring the water into every available empty pot, she hurried out to get some more. This time she was not so lucky.

She had gone only a few yards when she heard the noises: some men were loudly cursing and thumping upon the pavement with their sticks. What had happened was that earlier, hearing her in the lane, many of her neighbours had watched from behind closed doors and windows as she had gone by and then come back with water. They decided it was an opportune moment. Many of the people in the lane had always got most of their water from the public tap. By the time the old woman started again, several men and women had arrived at the tap, attracting the attention of a police party on patrol. But the people's need for water was so critical that, despite the curses and blows they immediately began to receive from the police, they did not run away. They hopped around, stumbled and fell, but kept pushing their pots under the gushing tap. Only when a pot was half full did its owner grab it and fly home. The old woman tried to be clever and, in all the confusion, managed to get both her buckets filled; but as she turned to go back, a policeman's swinging lathi hit the buckets and most of the water spilled out. She had to run home with what was left.

At home, she took out her chagrin on Sayeeda, who was still squatting against the wall, softly wailing, and had done nothing else. The old woman scolded her in her harshest voice, 'Karamjali! Still sitting there! There's still so much to be done. You think some maid will do it for you? Get up! . . . Quick!'

Sayeeda had always been scared of her. The effect of the old woman's words was that by the time the latter came back after keeping the buckets in the veranda, Sayeeda was standing up. The old woman went on muttering loudly, but Sayeeda did not give her another chance and staggered away to the latrine. When she returned, her mother-in-law had done much of the work and was now busy making a shroud out of a tattered sheet that had once been white. It had been a big relief to her to have found it at the bottom of one of her battered boxes. Sayeeda sat down close to her and stretched out her hand to help her, but the moment Sayeeda's hand touched the cloth, her eyes welled up and she choked. The old woman gently pushed away her hand and gestured to her own daughter, who grabbed Sayeeda in her embrace and pulled her all the way back. Now again Sayeeda leaned against the wall and watched in silence.

It took almost an hour to get everything ready. By the time the little body was washed and wrapped in the shroud, and a prayer was said, it was broad daylight. Finally the door was opened for the three men to go out with the corpse. Sayeeda was barely conscious, but she let out a shriek when the door was opened and, collapsing to the floor, began to wail aloud. She kept striking her head against the floor, Her husband was holding the shrouded baby. When he stepped out of the door, Sayeeda jumped up and ran after him. Suddenly, somehow, she had become so strong that her mother- and sister-in-law were dragged with her when they grabbed her arms to stop her.

At the door, with one foot outside and one twisted inside against the threshold, Sayeeda continued to wail, held back by the two women. The figures of the three men—heads bowed, one of them holding the little white bundle in his arms—disappeared around a corner. The doors and windows of the neighbouring homes that had opened partially were swiftly slammed shut. But who knew how many faces were pressed against them, peering out of little slits and holes?

It was 7.00 in the morning, and the sun was brilliant and rapidly warming up. The previous night had been too hectic, too tiring. One couldn't be sure, but it was most likely that breakfast had not yet been served in the homes of Haji Badruddin and Ramkrishna Jaiswal, and that the brimming buckets in the district officers' bathrooms were still waiting for them.

AFTERWORD

When I started working on *Curfew in the City,* I primarily used the experiences I had gained as a police officer during various communal riots. These experiences had an effect on me in two ways. As a police officer, I learned any number of useful professional tactics to employ on such occasions. At the same time, I was also exposed to many human tragedies hidden in these events—such as could inspire any writer. And that greatly helped me in writing this short novel and some shorter fictional pieces. In the Indian subcontinent, as elsewhere in the world, the worst suffering from communal violence is borne by the population's poorest and weakest, the most vulnerable sections. I learned this truth most forcefully as I performed my duties as an officer in an agency whose purpose is to establish and maintain peace.

When *Curfew in the City* was published in Hindi, it received a very diverse reception, and certain circles reacted to it quite strongly. That created in me a desire to study in a more organized manner the communalism that exists in the subcontinent, and its ugliest manifestation, the communal riot. Fortunately, I received a fellowship from the National Police Academy, Hyderabad, which made it possible for me to spend a year studying this most critical aspect of our contemporary society. The topic for my research was: 'The Perception of Police Neutrality during Communal Strife'. It chiefly meant a study of the role of the Indian police during communal riots, but I also used that time to study closely both the academic/theoretical and the more professional/prescriptive writings available on the subject of communalism. In what follows, I briefly try to share with my readers what I learned as a police officer during communal riots, what creative insights I gained as a writer from observing these immense human tragedies, and what I gained from my studies during that year. My hope is that these remarks will enable them to place this short novel in its wider context.

Let's first consider the reactions to the novel when it came out in 1987, for it will also help us gain some understanding of contemporary Indian society and the communalism that is rampant within it. Except for a small number of people who appreciated or criticized the book on purely literary grounds, the rest of the huge Hindi readership welcomed or condemned it simply on the basis of the community they belonged to.

It is an indisputable fact that in the riots that have occurred in India since Independence, Muslims account for more than 70 per cent of the fatalities. In the riots at Ranchi and Hatiya (1967), Ahmedabad (1969), Bhiwandi (1970), Jalgaon (1970) and Bombay (1992–93), as well as during the Ram Janmabhumi–Babri Mosque controversy and in the many riots all over the country subsequent to the destruction of the mosque, that percentage has in fact been above 90. And so it was natural that the Muslim readers of the novel in either Hindi or Urdu felt that it substantiated their conviction that they are always mistreated and discriminated against during riots. As a result, within a year several Urdu journals published translated versions of the novel, mostly without my knowledge or permission. I learned about them months, and in some cases years, later. Muslim reviewers and commentators showed particular enthusiasm in praising it. They, however, forgot to note as they applauded that the tragedy of the Muslims of India was exactly the same as that of the minorities in the other countries of South Asia. In fact, what has been happening to the Hindus of Pakistan and Bangladesh is perhaps much worse than what Indian Muslims have had to suffer. Even those Muslim communalist organizations which shamelessly preach the idea of establishing a Muslim state in a pluralistic society like India hugely publicized this novel in their journals. For me, as a writer, it was a very painful experience.

Converse to this response was the reaction of the fascistic proponents of Hindutva. They felt that this novel had placed the Hindus as guilty parties before the bar. Shri Ashok Singhal, head of the Vishwa Hindu Parishad, made the demand that the novel should be banned. He also announced that if any film were made based on the book, any cinema house that might show it would be torched. At the same time, I also received hundreds of letters in which I was cursed and denounced for writing an 'anti-Hindu' and 'pro-Muslim' novel.

I tried—both as a writer and as a Hindu—to examine and understand these diametrically opposite reactions, and pursued this matter with greater emphasis during the period of my fellowship. In time I came face-to-face with some very interesting facts.

When it considers the communal riots that happen here, the majority community in India ignores facts and appears obsessed with two preconceptions. An average Hindu believes (a) that the riots are started by the Muslims, and (b) that those who die in the riots are mostly Hindus.

The question of who starts the riots is arguable; however, the identities and numbers of those who are killed are absolutely not. Not only are more Muslims killed in almost all riots, they also account for more than 90 per cent casualties in more than half the riots. So, before talking about who starts the riot, let us first examine the figures for those who lose their lives.

The riots that have taken place in our country since 1960 are different in nature from the violence that occurred at the time of the Partition in 1947. By 1960, the causes that arose out of the Partition itself had by and large disappeared. If we set aside the few riots that took place as a reaction to the horrors recounted by Hindu refugees fleeing from the erstwhile East Pakistan, the causes for the remaining subsequent riots will appear to be quite unrelated to any memory of the Partition. These later riots took place either out of the efforts to reinvigorate Muslim and Hindu communal organizations that had lost their appeal in the immediate aftermath of the Partition or due to an increasing trend to use riots to garner political benefits. The official figures indicate that three-quarters of those who got killed in these riots were Muslims; likewise, 75 per cent of the property that was looted or destroyed belonged to the Muslims. Not only that, Muslims also accounted for a larger—unbelievably larger—percentage of those who were arrested for these riots.

Let us examine the casualty figures for a few major riots. The most terrible riot after 1960 occurred in Ahmedabad in 1969. According to the figures presented by the state government to the Inquiry Commission headed by Justice Jagmohan Reddy, 6742 houses or shops were burned down in that riot; out of them, only 671 belonged to Hindus, the remaining 6071 belonged to Muslims. The total value of the property destroyed in the riot came to Rs 4,23,24,068; out of it, the value of the property that belonged to Hindus was Rs 75,85,845, while the value of the property that belonged to Muslims was Rs 3,47,38,223. Of the 512 fatalities, 24 were Hindus, 413 were Muslims, while the remaining 75 could not be identified. The next major riot was at Bhiwandi in 1970, in which 78 persons were killed—of these, 17 were Hindus, 59 were Muslims, while 2 remained unidentified. It was disclosed in the statements made before the Inquiry Commission headed by Justice D.B. Madan that 6 Muslim women were raped during the riot, but no Hindu woman was so victimized. In the riot at Jalgaon that occurred as a consequence of the events at Bhiwandi, there were 43 casualties, of which one was a Hindu, the rest were all Muslims. Also at Jalgaon, the Muslims lost property worth Rs 33,90,977, while the Hindu losses came to Rs 83,725. Similarly, 184 persons were killed during the riots at Ranchi and Hatiya; among them 164 were Muslims, 19 were Hindus, while 1 could not be identified.

The above-mentioned riots were among the worst in India since 1960. In addition, there have been major riots at Jamshedpur, Aligarh, Varanasi and Bombay; there too the consequences were more or less the same. There was probably not a single riot where the percentage of Muslim casualties was lower than 70. The figures were the same with respect to the loss of property. The most amazing fact, however, is that, in almost every riot, the Muslims also formed the majority of the people taken into custody by the police. Likewise, it was mostly the Muslim homes that underwent searches. Apparently, even the police, like the majority community, think that Muslims are responsible for the riots and acts under the premise that the violence can be brought under control only by taking strong measures against Muslims.

The belief that there are more Hindu fatalities in the riots is so entrenched in the minds of the majority community that an average Hindu will not accept the fact that Hindus are the more aggressive party in these incidents. And when we probe this non-acceptance, we discover that it comes from certain underlying attitudes acquired in childhood. Every Hindu child is taught at home that Muslims are inherently cruel and do not hesitate to take a life, while the Hindus, conversely, are tender-hearted and find it hard to harm even an ant. Often you would come across a Hindu who would tell you, 'Arrey sahib, in a Hindu home you won't find any weapon except a little kitchen-knife to cut vegetables.' What this Hindu implicitly believes and is telling you is that Muslims commonly hoard weapons in their homes. And that is why, to an average Hindu, even the official figures for riot victims appear unacceptable, despite the fact that no government likes to put out figures that imply that the minorities in the country are not safe.

The other preconception that the majority community has concerns the question: Who starts the riots? It is a pervasive belief that in most such incidents the initiative is taken by the

Muslims. For a Hindu bureaucrat, educationist, journalist, jurist or policeman, it is only too easy to believe that it is the Muslims who start the riots. He makes that assertion in every conversation without a second thought. And the supporting argument that is commonly offered is that the riots generally begin in areas with a large Muslim population.

It was to make it easier to counter the above misconception that I began by raising the matter of who gets killed in the riots. There has not been a single riot in a hundred since 1960 in which the loss to Muslim life, property and 'honour' has been less in comparison. In most riots, not only did the Muslims suffer greater losses, but proportionately their losses were much higher than the Hindus'. Often more than 70 per cent of the total. And this is no secret either. Every Muslim knows that if a riot occurs, it is he who will be killed or have his property torched, and it is he who will also be arrested. He knows that similar things might possibly also happen to the Hindus, but in infinitely smaller measure. Why then, in such circumstances, would a Muslim start a riot? Is it that despite his being beaten down year after year his hunger for punishment does not die? Could it be that an entire community has decided to commit mass suicide? A laughable proposition, indeed, but that is not likely to have any effect on the thinking of an average Hindu.

The fact is that the answer to the question, 'Who started the riot?' is always sought by deciding who threw the first stone or who started the first fire. Such a conclusion is always wrong, for the way it is reached is itself incorrect. The people who have observed communal riots up close know that not every stone that is thrown succeeds in starting a riot. In fact, an air of tension is first created in the city before any riot occurs. And to that end—months before any incident—a web is woven of false accusations, rumours and negative propaganda. The tension keeps building up, until it reaches a flashpoint where just one stone or one inflammatory shouted slogan can cause a mighty explosion. And at that critical height of tension, it is immaterial who throws the first stone. What matters is the tense atmosphere. It is that which starts a riot; the stone or the slogan is merely an excuse.

To understand this matter better, let us examine the start of the communal riot that took place in Bhiwandi in 1970. It began on 7 May, when Muslims threw stones at the procession taken out to celebrate Shiva [Shivaji] Jayanti. And so, just by looking at the surface, it can be easily concluded that the Muslims started the riot. But if we look even a little deeper at the entire development of the incident, it becomes clear that such a conclusion is incorrect. Even before the actual riots occurred, there had already been a state of heightened communal tension in Bhiwandi for some time. As always, the Muslims had objected to the procession being taken past their mosque and to having the mosque and themselves spattered with colour. The local administration intervened and got the two parties to come to a workable compromise. The procession started. The people in the procession began to shout inflammatory slogans and, contrary to their promise, threw colour on the mosque. Consequently, the Muslims attacked the procession. Now if someone concludes from the latter that the riot was started by the Muslims, he is obviously disregarding the entire preceding series of events that raised tension to the point where even one stone could succeed in triggering a horrific riot.

More recently, during the riots in Hyderabad, it plainly emerged that the people in the procession itself could launch 'the first stone'. There, in a Hindu religious procession, some participants themselves threw stones at it. Since most of the other people in the procession remained ignorant of it, they easily assumed that the stones had come from the Muslims. That is how the riot started.

But, just for argument's sake, let us ignore the chain of events leading to the specific incidents that start riots. Let us try and explore that mental state itself in which the Muslims, on many occasions, throw the first stone and become the initiating cause. Most often that first stone is only the desperate reaction of a frightened and insecure community. This community, knowing well that all the loss will be its own, hits out first. Its poverty and lack of education and its blindly opportunistic leadership also play a large part in creating this reaction. It is no coincidence that the riots take place in those areas of a city where Muslims live in dense and filthy surroundings. Often their families, struggling against poverty and unemployment, do not even have enough space for all the members to sleep at the same time, and family members must take turns to snatch some rest. And their jobless youth become fertile ground for growing vagrancy and rumours.

Earlier I raised the question of the psychology of the majority community because without fully changing it, it wouldn't be possible to stop communal riots. The right-thinking members of the majority community will have to acknowledge that the victims of their aggression are repeatedly the members of the minority community; that the minorities have as much right to this land as they do; and that during periods of communal tension, the job of the police and the army is not to take the side of the majority community but to provide protection to the minorities. And that acknowledgement will come about only if there is a truly significant change in their thinking.

As for the Muslims of India, they too must use the issue of these riots to think about some other major questions. At the very beginning, they will have to acknowledge that the division of the country on the basis of the 'two-nation theory' was decidedly wrong. Hindus and Muslims cannot be two nations, nor can any nation be formed on the basis of religion alone. A Hindu and a Muslim of India who share the same social, economic and linguistic background are much closer to each other than any two other people who may share a common religion but do not share a common cultural heritage.

It would serve no purpose here to get involved in such questions as: 'Was the partition of India due only to the Muslims?' or 'How significant was their role in it?' or 'To what extent did contemporary Hindu intransigence force them into becoming partisans of the Partition?' Without getting entangled in such issues, the Muslims of India will have to acknowledge that the proposition that Hindus and Muslims are separate nations was put forward in its most emphatic form by their largest representative party, the Muslim League, and their biggest mass leader, M.A. Jinnah. If the Indian Muslims universally accept that the division of India was a mistake and that Hindus and Muslims are not two separate nations, it will greatly help us all to free ourselves from the terrible memories of the Partition.

Together with that, the Indian Muslims must also take note of an interesting but sad mindset. The tragedy is not just theirs, but of Muslims all over the world that wherever

Muslims are a minority they become the biggest champions of secularism and of the principle that the state must treat all its citizens alike. But the attitude changes wherever Muslims form the majority community; there they start believing in establishing an Islamic theocracy. It may sound hurtful but the truth is that the Indian Muslims have accepted secularism only as a matter of policy, and not as a matter of principle. As a matter of fact, this attitude has caused the greatest damage to those progressive elements among the Hindus that have been fighting the rising tide of Hindu fascism. These progressive Hindus are constantly challenged within their own community with the question: 'Why should only the Hindus remain secular, and for how long?' The Muslims must realize that the battle for secularism cannot be fought in parts, that there is a need to make the entire world secular, liberal and tolerant. This world of ours contains both Islamic and non-Islamic societies.

Curfew in the City is a short novel, but it gave me a lot of trouble as I wrote it. Most of its characters and incidents are connected with a small neighbourhood in Allahabad, and it was in the riots of 1980 that I first came to know them. Their pain was so immense that it seemed impossible to me to express it in words. Frequently I felt that the right words had slipped away from me, and that I had failed to write down what I had seen and felt. Of course, it has been said that language is a poor substitute for thought. Now the novel is in your hands. If this book enables even one reader to feel the hurt of Sayeeda and Devi Lala, or dream of a world that would not allow any riots to occur, or feel intense hatred for the elements that engineer riots—then I will feel that my efforts were not in vain.